2-

THE DARTMOOR YANKEE

THE DARTMOOR YANKEE

Malcolm Lynch

TABB HOUSE

First published 1992
Tabb House, 7 Church Street, Padstow, Cornwall, PL28 8BG

Copyright © Malcolm Lynch 1992

Paperback ISBN 0 907018 98 X
Hardback ISBN 0 907018 68 8

Typeset by St George Typesetting, Redruth Cornwall
Printed and bound by the Short Run Press Ltd., Exeter, Devon

Author's Note

In the midsummer of 1812 The United States of America declared war on Great Britain. Britain was at the time heavily involved in the war against Napoleon. Congress gave as its reason for the declaration of war the British Navy's confiscation of their merchant ships and the impressment of Yankee sailors into naval service. In reality, President James Madison had hoped to conquer Canada and add it to the rapidly expanding territories of the United States.

A peace treaty was signed on Christmas Eve 1814 with neither side winning or losing. It was known as the war that nobody wanted.

From the beginning of this war nearly nine thousand Yankee prisoners of war were incarcerated in Dartmoor Prison, which had been specially built in 1806 for French prisoners.

All the events, and characters and names of characters are true, and taken from prisoners' own accounts. So soon after the War of Independence the ex-colonials did not have a true identity and referred to themselves as Yankees.

The chapter titles are taken from *Magnalia Christi Americana*, by the American Puritan Cotton Mather (1663 – 1728), and would have been well known to any Harvard student in the eighteenth and early nineteenth centuries.

The story of the two lovers is fictitious.

Contents

CHAPTER ONE

Temptations of a Wilderness

THE young man hid behind the tall upright column of rock. There were nine of these primitive columns forming a circle, and he had dodged from one to the other until he was now behind the one nearest a small stone cottage. It was hot midsummer which was good, for he had been able to bury his yellow jacket, leaving him in his coarse, rough-spun shirt and trousers, and their grey colours had blended in with the moorland. No movement came from the cottage, yet instinct told him there was somebody inside. He would have to wait.

The silence was shattered by the sudden bursting into song of a skylark. The song was everywhere, yet above him. It filled the sky and pierced his brain. He looked up, and there was the small bird fixed in the blue sky with its quivering wings. The heat of the day may have numbed the skylark's awareness; way, way above it another bird was fixed higher in the sky. A large buzzard hovered in the warm upcurrent. The buzzard dropped on the singing bird, there was a quick, sharp squawk of pain and death, and the singing stopped. The buzzard circled gracefully upward again, and disappeared with its prey on top of a black stone tor.

A young woman came out of the door. She wore a loose, long frock, and although it was too big for her it curved round the shapes of her beautiful body. He was twenty-six; she was about nineteen or twenty. Her face was perfect: a slightly turned-up nose, a broad forehead, a small chin, and red hair which although unkempt was a glory.

He'd seen pretty girls before and had always had to look away from them out of shyness, but this girl could not see him. He could steal her beauty.

1

She took an axe and cut up some dried branches that were heaped outside the cottage. A dozen hens rushed to her and pecked her round ankles. She carried the wood inside, and some of the hens followed her, clucking for their corn. Shortly, blue smoke curled up from the chimney, and she came out again with a bowl of corn, which she scattered to the hens.

After that, she took a space and turned over clods of turf so that they would dry in the sun. During her chores she turned and twisted and bent her body so that every curve and bend of her delightful figure was tantalisingly but momentarily displayed. The effect on the peeping man was so powerfully physical that he would not have cared if a redcoat had crept up behind him and driven a bayonet between his shoulder-blades. Indeed he romantically thought of a swift death, for it didn't seem right to him that a man should see such bewitching beauty and live. Had she been a Medusa, he would not have minded.

There was a well encircled by a small stone wall and above it a wooden beam from which a large iron bucket was suspended. The young woman lowered the bucket, and the handle and chain creaked. It stopped creaking and she wound it up again, resting a foot on the wall to give her extra strength. Then she lugged the overflowing bucket towards the house.

"You can come out from behind that rock, mon ami!" she said calmly and sweetly. "Your breakfast will soon be ready!"

He was petrified; he couldn't move. She couldn't be talking to him, she couldn't see him.

She sighed and raised her arms in a gesture of mock despair. "Ah well, if you want to stay behind the stone, it's up to you," she went on. "But you'll be letting a good breakfast go to waste. And there ain't no redcoats waiting for you. This ain't no trap. There's only me. Je suis seule, mon brave."

He came out from behind the rock. It mattered little if there were a dozen redcoats with loaded muskets trained on him, he had to go towards her. He would hold her and kiss her, and the redcoats could fire a volley.

She smiled at him; it was so magnetic a smile it was as though her lips pulled him towards her. She walked into the cottage, and he followed her. The scrubbed white table was laid out for a meal.

2

"Eh, voila, m'sieur! A tankard of elderberry wine, and eggs, goat's cheese, rabbit and dandelions – all fried to a turn. And some whortleberries and cream. Bien, n'est-ce pas?"

"I'm not a Frenchman."

"You're wearing prisoner-of-war clothing. You've escaped from Dartmoor Prison." She had the hint of a lisp in her sweet voice.

"I've escaped from the prison. But I'm a Yankee."

"Well, goodness gracious me! I ain't ever seen no Yankee before in all my born days."

She walked round him, weighing him up with her eyes.

"You look same as any other man. And whatever is a Yankee doing up at the new war prison, if I may make so bold as to ask, kind sir?"

"America has declared war on England. The English were seizing our ships and pressing our crews into their navy. I had a ship, my own ship, which plied trade between Boston and Bristol. I was peaceful and unarmed, then an English frigate threatened to sink me with all hands. What could I do? I had to lower the flag. And that's what one Yankee is doing up at the war prison, and there are hundreds of us."

"So you're an enemy?"

"I guess that's the word you'd use."

"But tell me . . ." She held her finger to her lips as though deep in thought. "Do you not think I am pretty?"

He was flabbergasted at such a surprise question. He had expected to be asked more about himself. "Why – yes!"

"You do not say so. All you do is talk about yourself."

"I think you're pretty."

"Do you not want to kiss me?"

"Desperately."

"Do all Yankees talk as much as you do?"

He held her and kissed her. The world was his. It was his first ever time. But this should not happen in England, the land of the oppressor, it should happen in Boston after marriage in a church.

"Beloved enemy!" she whispered in his ear before kissing him on the lips. Her lips were sweet and perfumed with the taste and aroma of freshness. "Do you surrender?"

3

"Oh yes," he gasped.

"I think you're a very friendly foe. A Yankee, eh?"

"From Boston, Massachusetts."

"Masser — what?"

"New England."

"Well then, a brand-new Englishman all to myself, and from a new England. 'Tis time they was making new ones, if you ask me: the old ones are very old and worn. But you talk like you was nobility."

"I went to Harvard. It's a college."

"Did you now? And where did all that college learning get you, eh? Dartmoor Prison. You're frightened of me, aren't you?"

"No – overwhelmed."

He was overwhelmed. He was weak and timid with wonder, as though he had stumbled across the back gate to heaven. For two days after he'd escaped from prison he'd followed sheep-tracks up and down the high, rugged hills. He'd been lost, lost utterly and entirely, lost to the world. He'd not eaten, and he'd trudged on expecting to collapse and die on the moor like he'd been told so many escaped prisoners had done. And then this free-and-easy, lovely angel. He had entered the back gate of heaven, of that there was no doubt.

"What did they teach you at Harvard?" she asked.

"Nothing," he said.

"Well, come to the college of Dartmoor." She waved around the room. "It'll teach you to survive. It'll make a man of you. It'll finish off your education. Won't that be magic?"

She got up and walked to the door.

"Where are you going?" he asked.

"To collect the eggs, to milk the goats, to get some turf for the fire, then I got to see to the horses, then I got to get sheep-fat to make candles. But it won't take me long, and there'll be all day and all night, and a million days and nights, you see. Here, drink some gorse wine made from the yellow blooms o' the gorse, and the only true drink for lovers." She placed a flagon on the floor beside him.

"I don't know your name," he said.

"Now that's funny, cos I don't know yours. You could be the

King of England. Shows how I trust you." And she stepped out.

He filled his tankard and looked around the room. There were many shelves on the wall, and they were filled with earthenware jars, one or two of them bubbling; he guessed they were wines in the making. Other jars gave off pleasant smells and were surrounded by wasps; they would be jams. The walls were of grey granite rocks. On the small window-ledge, and on smaller ledges in the walls, were jars of gorse twigs in bloom. There were no pictures, there was no clock. Time evidently did not exist.

He looked through the window out onto the great hills. One or two of the larger hills had gigantic rocks on their crests. These he'd been told were called tors, and they made unearthly shapes; one heap of rocks took on the shape of a ruined castle, another could have been a devil's head, another a giant wolf. At the side of one tor was a herd of wild ponies. They hardly moved as they munched the tough grass and heather. Time for them did not exist.

The girl returned to put turf on the fire.

"Never let the fire go out on the moor, or you'll die of cold."

"My name is John Adams," he said.

"Of New England," she replied. "Now I know all about you. Ain't you important?"

"What's your name?"

"Sally."

"Sally what?"

"That's a nice name. Sally what. I think I'll call myself Sally What."

"Your Christian name."

"Oh, I haven't got a Christian name. I don't think I deserve a Christian name."

"You must have parents."

"Most people has parents, don't they? I don't know my parents. Let's say my mother was a tor and my father was the north wind. Let's say that, eh?"

"I like Sally."

"I like John Adams."

"New England is full of Adamses."

"Well, we have to thank King George and King Madison for bringing a new English Adams to Dartmoor."

5

"Madison?"

"Yes, Madison. Why do you ask?"

"Because you're not just a simple country girl. Not many in in this country know who Madison is."

"I never said I was a simple country girl. I live here and make money by selling horses and sea passages to French officers on parole."

"Then you're a spy."

"An Englishman would call me a spy, but then you're not an Englishman, are you?"

"My grandparents were. I'm not."

"I'm Cornish. Do you know what that is?"

"Not really."

She laughed. "Cornwall is the other side of the hills. We're not English. We have the same original language as the French in Brittany. We are closer to the French than we are to the English. Is that being a spy or a traitor?"

"I guess not."

"Good – then stay with me."

"I'm here to escape, Sally. If possible to regain my ship and go home."

"A ship!" she scorned. "Puff – what's a ship? Pieces of wood blown along by an old maid's petticoat. Stay here, my love, and I'll teach you to make things happen."

"You already have done. Tell you what – I'll take you back to Boston with me."

She laughed and showed a thin row of white teeth. She looked lovely when she did so.

"Me – in Boston? Can you imagine me in Boston? I wouldn't survive in Boston. I belong to the moor."

"But sooner or later the English will capture you."

"The English will never capture me. They may capture you but they will never capture me."

There were a few minutes' silence. Outside in the evening landscape owls hooted and gave their sudden hunting shriek, and somewhere among the tors a fox barked.

"Sally, don't you have a husband, a lover, a friend?"

"I have no husband and no friends. But I have lovers, dashing

6

French lieutenants and brave captains. Yes, I am all you think I am. Do you wish to leave? I can find you a horse?''

"No, I don't wish to leave. But are you safe here?''

"Don't you mean are *you* safe? No matter. Of course I'm safe. Nobody would ever come to my valley. It leads to nowhere, to no towns. And on Dartmoor, no one ever leaves the tracks or trails. I can show you skeletons of those who did.''

"No, thank you!''

"I sell a few horses at Moreton to French officers on parole. They pay a lot of money. Très charmant.'' She kissed him. "Je t'aime, ma chéri!''

"They say things like that to you?''

"How else would I know the words? Besides, why should it bother you, John, for 'tis over the waves to New England for you. Isn't that right?''

"I guess so.''

Her eyes looked towards the window as though aware of approaching danger. She put her hand over John's mouth.

"Hush! Can you hear him? 'Tis Reynard after my precious hens. If I've told him once I've told him a thousand times to leave my hens alone, but will he take heed? He will not. One of these fine nights I'll have to shoot him.'' She fumbled under the bed and brought out a pistol and rod and a bag of powder and shot.

"I'll bring a candle,'' he said.

"Why waste sheep-grease when there's a moon.''

She crept out of the room, and then he heard her voice.

"Yes, I thought t'was you. After my hens again, eh? Never mind looking at me like that. And don't pretend you wasn't after my cockadoodles. Now, skit-skat-scoot! Away with you or I'll shoot your tail off. Allez-vous-en!''

Sally returned to the bedroom. "Sneaky little devil, he is.'' Then she levelled the pistol at John's chest and cocked it. "How d'y'know I'm not a fox, John? Cunning as a fox, isn't that what they say? You can't trust me, John, no more'n I can shoot you and sling you over a horse and take you back to the war prison and say you attacked me. And they'll maybe give me a shilling, that's what they pay for turning in French prisoners. I don't know what the going rate for Yankees is. What d'y'reckon a dead Adams is

7

worth? Ten a penny in New England, so you said.''

John moved towards her. ''Give me that pistol. It might go off!'' She handed him the pistol. ''I'll say this, John. You're no coward. Shoot me! Go on, love – shoot me. Let it end tonight. This is a good night for it to end. You'll find money in them vases, plenty of money, and you can pick the finest horse to ride. I don't want to lose you, but time will steal you away. Finish it. Better to be shot by a man who loves you than by a man who hates you. You'll carry me in your memory for all your life, and I'd like that.''

She fell in his arms. He let the pistol drop to the floor to embrace her. The pistol exploded, and for a second they both thought they were shot. Then they burst out laughing, and when they'd finished laughing, they kissed quietly; a deep, in-breathing, sweet, joined together, merging kiss.

''We're mad,'' she whispered.

John lived the life of a primitive man except that he shaved. Sally, from one of her oak chests, found him a dagger which she told him had been made in the same forge in France where they made the guillotine blades. If the blade-edge was sharp enough to remove the head of a duke, she said, it was fine enough to take the whiskers away from a Yankee.

It was a life of summer sunshine and abundance; there was never any shortage of food. Sometimes he caught trout in the River Dart which wandered through the valley; sometimes he snared rabbits. They saw not a soul.

He dug turf and stacked it, and chopped wood, and raised the heavy bucket from the well. She busied herself with cooking, gathering herbs, and brewing wine and beer. She also fed and took care of her small herd of horses which were kept in a rough stockade in the next valley. They all galloped towards her when she whooped, and she could jump on the back of any horse and ride it. John tried to ride them but was thrown and bruised. They slept among the heather in the sunshine in the afternoons; their nights were wild with love, and they often saw the red dawn.

But on some days when he sat on the banks of the rushing river

8

waiting for a fish to bite, he worried. This was all new and strange to him. He had never loved before, but now he loved Sally. She was wild, and she had been carefree with men. It was an exciting kind of love which made the heather tingle and the ground springy to his feet. The fresh air filled his lungs to near bursting-point and sometimes he thought he was going to burst with love and pride. He was her man of the moment, but only of the moment. He was her man, but was she his woman? It would still end in a thunderstorm and he would be stricken with a thunderbolt, of that he was convinced. This life could not last. It was as though he had gone back a thousand years, yet his brain was branded with civilisation. He came from a big house on Beacon Hill, and there were servants. The sedate ladies at Chestnut wore fashionable dresses with poke bonnets and silk ribbons. They held on to their husbands' arms and made smiling curtsies when they met in the tree-lined streets, and their husbands raised their tricorn hats with sweeping gestures. It was ironic that the great Adams family, the pride of New England, had gone to the New World from Somerset, the next county to the one in which he was now a fugitive. He thought of Harvard's two colleges; he had resided in the one with the dome. He remembered the songs of the Cambridge taverns; he remembered the smell of the books and the wax polish, the sound of the chapel bell, the shape of maple leaves. His parents had wanted him to become a clergyman, but he'd wanted the unrestricted freedom of thought, which was why he'd gone to sea. He preferred the sharp satires of John Dryden to the November sky heaviness of the Puritan Cotton Mather; his Bible was the autobiography of Benjamin Franklin. Nevertheless, Boston was his world, though he doubted if it could ever become Sally's. She would not suit Boston, and Boston would undoubtedly not suit her.

A beautiful compromise sprang to his mind and it made him yippee with the sheer joy of inspiration. West was the answer, west beyond the mountains and the big wide river. He would return to America with Sally and they would head out for the unmapped, unpeopled Wild West territories of the sunset. Yes, that would suit Sally; it was a wilderness ten thousand times more vast than Dartmoor.

9

He told her of his dream, and she agreed.

"Then we'd better go to Exeter and arrange for a ship," she said.

"A ship costs money."

"I've got money."

"But it's not mine."

"Don't be silly, it's ours. It's the price of a new life with freedom."

"Let's go, then."

"Friday."

"Why Friday? Why not now?"

"Because there's a hanging on Friday, most Fridays, and I've been to many a hanging, and they're very enjoyable."

Often her hardness frightened him; she would talk to a rabbit before she killed it; and yet there were times when she could be more gentle than he thought possible. Usually she showed her tenderness when he'd been stung by a wasp, and there were a lot of wasps and he was stung a lot of times; because of her jams, wines and herbs, the tiny cottage was like a wasps' nest. He was often stung on his backside when they were making love. Sally told him they were the souls of dead redcoats who had been killed by Yankees, and they were revenging themselves by stinging him with their tiny bayonets. He told her that he didn't believe so many Englishmen had been or could be killed by Yankees. When he'd been thus wounded by the stab of a vengeful redcoat, she dabbed the part with a concoction of herbs, and nursed him and cuddled him as though he were a baby; she even spoonfed him with mutton broth, and she sang him lullabies. He relished every minute of this mollycoddling; her hands were so gentle, her lips were so sweet.

He awoke before daylight on Friday. He woke up because his body missed the comfort of her body, she had left the bed. The door was open, and he tiptoed through. The air outside on the moor was good, and there was a soft breeze caused by the darkness of the night being chased by the approach of morning. There was a hint of the sea in the breeze.

Her white and perfect body stood out against the greyness of the dawn. She stood motionless in the centre of the circle of stones.

10

The stones stood out deep black and the morning star flashed blue and bright from the eastern sky. Sally was facing the east; he saw her beautiful profile silhouetted by a faint glow from the distant sea. Not even a gentle breathing rhythm came from her breasts; she was as still as a statue.

John stared and for some reason his thoughts went back to Harvard. He had delivered a dissertation in the great hall, to the annoyance of some tutors, to the delight of others. He had attacked the fanciful notions of Bishop Berkeley, who had held that this was not a materialistic world, that all observed objects were merely ideas in the mind of the beholder, put there by the imagination of God. He had defended the philosophy of Isaac Newton, who held that everything was mathematically explainable; it was a universe of mathematics, a world without illusion or magic. The learned men of New England's past had believed in the existence of necromancy, of witches and witchcraft, but he'd refuted them and their superstitions. But now the lovely statue standing among the stones in the lightening dawn could be nothing else but a bewitching vision. His life with Sally was enchanting, and yet there were moments when he longed to be back in the safety and security of the prison.

The sky became brighter, and the thin red curve looked over a straightness which was the sea. Red wisps of cloud ribbed the sky, now growing blue. John tiptoed back to bed and pretended to be asleep. After a time, Sally joined him. She stroked his hair and whispered: "No, I'm not a witch, darling." He felt a shiver run down his spine; it was as though she had read his thoughts. "I'm just a girl who needs your help, as you need mine. Maybe some day you'll understand."

After breakfast she selected two fine horses, which she said would fetch a good price in Exeter. She also brought two sacks of clothing from one of her chests, one of which she handed to John.

"There's fine clothes for a gentleman," she said. "But before we put them on, we'll go for a swim."

John had become a good horseman, and they galloped fast to the river. She pointed down into the rushing waters.

"See that big round stone under the water, John? Well that's what they call the dollymin stone and there's a big hole right through the centre which'll just allow two bodies to wriggle through together, and I want you to swim through with me. Will you, John?''

The thought of plunging into a deep, fast-flowing and turbulent mountain river, then wriggling through a hole in a rock, was daunting to John, but he trusted her. The current was fierce but clear; so clear that the tiniest brown pebble could be seen changing shape, and the crystal clarity of the river threatened an icy coldness. Naked, they plunged in and fought the current to reach the stone, otherwise the current would have taken them headlong into the rock. John reached it first and pulled Sally towards it, then clutching each other tightly they wriggled through the hole in the rock with a great deal of difficulty. John thought they would never get their hips through, that the stone would hold them in its grip until they drowned; but just when his lungs were fit to burst, he broke through. They reached the surface and took loud and big gasps of air, then they crawled, as weak as half-drowned kittens, on to the bank.

''Now there we are – we're married now. And 'tis the only proper way to be married, through danger. Maybe some day you'll give me a golden wedding-ring, and the ring will signify what we've just been through together. Isn't that so, John, my darling? Tell me now!''

He told her it was so, and he believed it was so. He was flushed with pride at what he thought was a great achievement, swimming in a raging current through the dollymin stone, risking his life for the woman he loved. He wondered if it had been like this in the Garden of Eden; he felt as though he were dwelling in the Garden of Eden, and that he and Sally were the only two people in the world; how else could Adam and Eve have gotten married? There was no clergyman and no church; there had been only God, and he wasn't too favourably inclined towards them. John was amused by his thoughts but nevertheless believed in a certain amount of logic in them.

''Come on, let's put our clothes on,'' Sally said, rummaging in the bags. ''Here's some fancy pantaloons, and a shirt trimmed with lace, and a green velvet jacket. Won't you be the handsome one in Exeter? Keep your eyes off the wenches though, for there's some pretty wenches in Exeter." She stood back and admired him.

"Oh là là! Très magnifique!"

"For heaven's sake, Sally, you don't have to speak French! You don't have to remind me."

She shook a leather bag of money under his nose.

"If it wasn't for them French officers buying my horses and paying me for my help, we wouldn't be going to America, my darling. They're your allies. They're your fellow-prisoners. You're fighting each other's battles. Vive Napoléon!"

John looked disdainfully at the purse. "Money!" he sneered.

"Well, maybe, witch as you seem to think I am, we should fly there on my broomstick, or I should wave my magic wand." She suddenly slapped her horse. "To Exeter! Giddy-up!" And away she raced with the horse's tail high. John followed her full pelt.

They stabled their horses at a Tudor inn just outside the town. Sally paid the hostlers, then she took John's arm to walk through the streets, and John was able to admire her. She wore a blue dress with a white sash round her waist; over her red hair she wore a wide-brimmed hat in blue, trimmed with a red band, and a white rose clasped under the band. Men looked twice at her – and she smiled back, to John's chagrin. Women looked at her, then looked the other way. She was easily the most beautiful and ladylike woman in the town, and John knew it. She was worth ten thousand dollymins.

He felt the cobblestones tingling to his shoes, and was as excited and nervous as a small boy in a new suit at a party. Yet there had been a time not so long ago when he'd been in command of his own ship, confident of his own navigation calculations, shouting compass directions to the helmsman, ordering the first mate to have the mizen trimmed or the mainmast spread, ploughing his ship through the high waves of a severe storm, or risking his hull in the shallows between rocks. But this confidence had gone, and now he depended upon the beautiful girl who held his arm.

"There's two of 'em to be hanged," said Sally. "Fetched in for stealing sheep, they was. It's a nice day for hanging, and the executioner will make 'em dance for us by putting the knot at the side of their necks so's they'll choke. If it was wet now, and not many people, he'd put the knot at the back, and snap their necks. There'll come a flute-player to play a merry jig while they dance.''

"It's barbaric.''

"Not that barbaric, darling. Them two men will be that excited that the crowds have turned out to watch them, although they may mess in their pantaloons and stink most terribly when they're being led past you.''

The crowds became thicker and the laughter louder. Salesmen and entertainers dodged between the carriages of the gentry. Beggars begged and men played fiddles, and there were fifes and drums on every corner. The air was warm and smelled of cheese, tobacco and hot meat pies.

A crowd gathered around two one-legged men who were clicking their wooden legs in a foot fight as bets were laid on them.

"You never lost your leg at Trafalgar, cos you wasn't bloody there!''

"And you didn't part with your leg on the Nile.''

"I bloody did.''

"You bloody didn't.''

"First to fall is a bloody liar and needs keelhauling.''

And the clicking of wooden legs became more furious to hurrahs of the crowd. A fiddler played a hornpipe.

There was another crowd around a tent which displayed an announcement that within was a real live cannibal king brought from the cannibal island, and it would cost half a penny to touch his belly.

"What's a cannibal? Does it mean he's swallowed a cannon-ball?'' asked a small boy, looking up at his mother.

"It means he eats little boys alive, especially little boys what stop to play when they should be carrying buckets of water from the pump.''

"Do you want to see the cannibal king?'' asked Sally with a wink.

"No, thanks. I've seen the commandant up at the prison, and that's enough man-eaters to last a lifetime.''

Hawkers sold dolls hanging from the gallows. They twirled them around.

"Dance little dolly, dance-a-pie!
Dance little dolly in the sky!"

One hawker, with a black patch over one eye, held out broadsheets, claiming it was a poem written by one of the condemned men only the night before:

"They say as bread is the staff of life,
So I stole a loaf for me and my wife.
Tomorrow I swing till I takes me last breath,
For the loaf what I stole was the staff of death."

Women sold flowers from baskets, others sang and held out their hands for money.

"Drink to me only with thine eyes,
And I will pledge with mine;
Or leave a kiss but in the cup,
And I'll not look for wine."

A little girl sang the song, and John, without permission, dipped into Sally's purse and gave the child a gold coin.

"Hey-up!" said Sally, "Or they'll think you're the Duke o' Devonshire. A gold piece indeed! Her mammy'll let you take her to bed and sing her a dozen lullabies for that kind of money."

John bent down and whispered in the child's ear, and the little girl sang:

"Of all the girls that are so smart,
There's none like pretty Sally,
She is the darling of my heart,
And she lives in our alley."

"That's why I gave her the money," said John. "Have you any complaints now?"

"Yes, a song about Sally ain't worth a gold guinea. Ain't worth even a farthing, and that's the truth."

Sally turned to smile and click her tongue at a man who patted

15

her bottom as he passed. "I must get to the prison in time," she said. "It would be terrible lonely for a body to be hanged without people there to watch and cheer." She squeezed his arm and looked up into his eyes, and he had to look away because she looked so beautiful.

"And after that, I'll go down to the quayside on my own and look up my friends and obtain a ship. I know the good captains from the bad 'uns. Don't forget 'tis my job to arrange things like this; they knows me. With you talking clever like you do, they'll not trust you. Might be one of His Majesty's spies, they'll think. So think on, you keep out of sight till it's nigh time to go on board."

John said he'd wait in a tavern.

"Ain't you just the limb of the very old Harry? Wait in a tavern! Wait in a tavern, be blowed! Hangings always bring the press-gangs to town, for the town fills up with lusty lads from the farms." She laughed. "Oh, you'll find a ship all right, with the help of a cudgel, a piece of sackcloth and some rope. Is that what you want? Of course it ain't. I got better plans for you than scrubbing decks. Listen to me, John Adams, away you go and look at the tombs in the cathedral. You'll be safe there."

"The cathedral?"

"Ay, the cathedral. It'll do you more good than harm, and I'll know where to find you. You know what a cathedral looks like, don't you? It's like a church that's grown old, and heavy and fat – like a church with gout."

"I'll find it."

"No need; it's found you. It's calling you. Harken!"

The bells had started pealing, and as John looked in the direction of the sound, he saw the two grey towers looming up above the clusters of Tudor shops.

"And that's a good omen," said Sally, smiling. "Au revoir!"

She walked down the road towards the prison, and John strode up the road towards the ringing bells.

As he walked in through the arched great door, he felt as small as Gulliver in the land of Brobdingnag. He had never been in a cathedral before and was overawed by the height. People coughed from secret corners, and there seemed to be a smell of incense

16

lingering from over three hundred years back in time. He wondered if his America would survive long enough to grow cathedrals. Right now, its chances were slim. Just fancy, his ancestors had originated in the next shire, the shire of Somerset. Maybe hundreds of years ago there had been occasions for them to take horse and carriage to Exeter to attend some grand function, perhaps a wedding – yes, a wedding. A wedding between Sir John Adams, clad in Arthurian armour, and Lady Sally, all in white with a white conical head-dress from which a veil flowed; the kind of maiden who was saved from dragons. A carved frieze near the high roof caught his eye. It was a band of musicians, perhaps angels, perhaps not, playing their harps, lutes and trumpets. He imagined they were playing 'Yankee Doodle' and nearly laughed out loud. The Arthurian spell was broken.

In a pew against a tomb of a mitred bishop, an old man supped from the neck of a flagon, then looked furtively around before putting the flagon back on the floor, holding his finger to his lips with a shush-it's-a-secret gesture to the stone bishop.

In another pew, a woman munched greedily at half of a large meat pie. A small boy at her side just held his half without attempting to eat it. "Now come on, son," she said, nudging him with her elbow. "Eat your pie all up, what the good lady gave us. One of the gentlemen out there being sent to heaven is your father, and after today it'll be the poorhouse for me and the orphanage for you, and there won't be no pig pies like the one we've got. So if you can't say a prayer for your father what's being hanged, at least you can eat your pig pie."

In a pew nearby, a young woman with a flower basket on the seat fumbled with her skirts as she adjusted her stockings. When she saw John looking, she raised her skirts to show her thighs. "Take a look, Billy boy! Ain't no charge for just a-looking! Pretty limbs, eh?" She gave her thigh a resounding slap, which caused the man with the flagon to turn round in his pew and do a shush with his finger to his lips.

John was embarrased. He felt that Sally, when she returned to him, would know he had looked at another woman's thighs. He moved down the aisle to read the epitaphs; there might even be an Adams on one of them. There was. It was a sad story of three

17

brothers drowned in a shipwreck. A frightening sensation that he himself had struck against the rocks came over him when a hand gripped his arm. He turned round to see a dirty, unshaven face with a scar, which made the man appear to be snarling. "Got any tobacco on you, matey?" the man asked.

"Sorry – no!"

"Got the price of a plug then, matey?"

"No!"

"Then may you rot in hell!"

"I probably shall," answered John. "In which case I'll keep a weather-eye open for you."

John found the darkest corner and sat down. He tried to pray but couldn't. He used to pray when he went with his parents to the old north church in Boston – or perhaps he had never prayed. He couldn't remember. He recalled his father telling him that this was the church upon which Paul Revere had lighted two lanterns to warn the people of Charleston that the British were coming. The wooden-faced church had a slender white steeple, and it had been the first church in Boston to ring a peal of bells, a gentle peal, unlike the heavy tolling that had started above the cathedral. The English bells were hoarse with shouting and commanding, like an old man who shouts at his grandchildren. Just outside the dainty Boston church, in the square, was the silversmith Paul Revere's house, and his father always saluted it on his way home. It was a relief to wait outside the church, for the sermons went on for hours. He remembered now: he didn't pray; he used to think of Paul Revere. And Benjamin Franklin. Now, there was a man! If only Benjamin Franklin were alive today! He would raise money to build a cathedral in Boston and pack it with people, and he would go round with the collection-trays and make a lot of money for the cathedral. But Benjamin Franklin had died over twenty years ago. John looked up at the musicians frieze again, and once more pretended they were playing 'Yankee Doodle'. He tried to shake off his fantasies. He wasn't a fantasy man, he was a mathematical man in a mathematical world, the world of Isaac Newton. He directed his thoughts to the medieval stonemasons who had chiselled the statues with such precision and craftmanship. Labour and achievement, that's what the world was about, and he didn't want to think of the Exeter bells shouting down the Boston bells, or of the cathedral statues playing 'Yankee Doodle'.

The deep, sonorous tolling of the bell stopped, and the dark of the belfry seemed to press down on John. Outside in the sunshine the two men had stopped dancing and were now hanging stiff from the gallows. Sally would be coming for him soon, and she would not find him hidden away in a dark corner, so he stepped up towards the high altar. He sat in a pew near the altar, and waited and waited. Even though close to the altar, he still couldn't pray. He filled his brain with what substituted for prayers by guessing the height of the towers, the breadth of the cathedral at its widest part, the depth of the cathedral's foundations, the approximate year when the cathedral was founded.

He felt Sally slide next to him. "Missed me?" she asked.

"It was eternity."

"Good."

"What's good about it?"

"That you missed me."

"I love you."

"Careful! You're saying that before the altar of a cathedral. You best mean it. You never know who's listening."

"I love you again and again. Let the bells ring!"

"Well, follow me. No time to lose."

She bustled him out of the pew, although by now he had developed a reluctance to leave the cathedral; he could have stayed with Sally in the gloom for ever.

She gripped his arm and led him down the main aisle, and they walked out through the main door into dazzling sunshine which nearly blinded him, although not so much that he couldn't see a line of redcoats with muskets pointed towards him.

"That's him!" shouted Sally, and she let go of his arm and walked away from him. "That's the Dartmoor Yankee!"

CHAPTER TWO

Kennels of Wolves

"YOU damned Bible-thumpers of the so-called States of America know your John Bunyan, of that I'm sure. Well, this is Doubting Castle and I'm Giant Despair. If I had my way, Mr Adams, I'd have you shot before an execution squad. You're a bloody deserter!"

"With respect, Captain Cotgrave, I'm a prisoner of war, and I escaped, which is the natural inclination of all prisoners of war. You would have done the same."

"Prisoner of war, my arse! You damned Yankees are nothing but Englishmen gone wrong: bent, twisted, stinking rotten, failed Englishmen; rebels, traitors, fratricides, the throw-away rubbish of English parents, colonial bastards. I was at Yorktown when the band played."

"It was your band. You called the tune."

Captain Cotgrave began turning the pages of a large ledger. "Every name in this ledger is an English name, and yours heads the alphabet."

John Adams stood in the commandant's office between two soldiers, both wearing different uniforms. One soldier's nose twitched, until he rubbed it with his sleeve. The other soldier wiggled his foot as though something were climbing up his leg.

Cotgrave prodded them. "Just look at these two, will you, Mr Adams. They're supposed to be specimens of the greatest army in the world."

John wondered if Captain Cotgrave considered himself to be a specimen of the greatest navy.

He had a sea-boot on one foot, a buckled shoe on the other. His trousers were baggy and stained, a pocket of his dirty blue

20

tunic was torn. He had the round face with the round red nose of a port-wine drinker. There was an unpowdered grey wig on the side of his head, one of the small black ribbons of which was undone. He repeatedly took snuff from the back of his hand, and sniffed it up with loud noises. It was enough to make a horse sneeze, but it had no effect on Captain Cotgrave. He was an old man and had a limp.

Rumour had it that he had once been charged with piracy on the high seas, but the charge had not been proved. Nevertheless, he had not been given another ship, and had been transferred to shore duty as commandant of Dartmoor War Prison.

The walls of his office were large blocks of Dartmoor granite, its only decoration an old and tattered British flag which did not have the diagonal red cross of Ireland. There were several tables stacked high with leaning, higgledy-piggledy columns of ledgers.

He prodded the open ledger with a thick finger. ''That's right, top o' the list. Adams – begins with an A. Boston, Massachusetts. Master of the *Boston Trader*.''

''That's right. Trader begins with a T.''

''Thank you! Any relation to John Adams, who called himself President twelve years ago?''

''Distant.''

''I thought so. A family of rebels. I put in at Pitcairn Island some years ago, and the leader of them mutinous dogs from the *Bounty* was John Adams too. Tarred with the same brush, all you Adamses. I might as well have you shot and be done with it.''

''I was plying my peaceful trade when a man-o'-war confiscated my vessel and took me and my crew prisoners. That's hardly mutiny or rebellion.''

''Plying your peaceful trade, eh? Taking a cargo to France to succour the King's enemies. What should we have done – offered to escort you safely to a French port?''

''The French are not the enemies of my country.''

''Don't be too sure about that, Mr Adams. Have you the slightest idea what your war of rebellion and this present Madison skirmish are all about? Have you?''

''Life, liberty and the pursuit of happiness,'' said John.

Captain Cotgrave burst out laughing. He slapped his thighs and strode towards the soldiers, giving them each a thump on the arm. "Laugh when the Yankee makes a joke!" he shouted. "Laugh or you'll be cleaning out shit-houses for the next twelve months."

The two soldiers forced noises which could be taken for laughs.

"A Jeffersonian parrot, Mr Adams, that's what you are, and you deserve to be kept in a cage and fed nuts. Listen and I'll tell you, and you'll be a wiser man than most of your countrymen." He went back to his table, adjusted his wig, and glanced up at the flag on the wall. "We gave the colonists money to start their businesses, and we guaranteed to purchase all they could produce. And our soldiers gave their lives protecting you from the French and their Indians out of Canada. We beat the French and Canada became ours, and you were no longer in danger; so, feeling safe and secure, you mutinied because you wanted more money for your products, and you didn't feel inclined to contribute any small share towards the conquest of Canada. And now that our hands are tied behind our backs in a life-and-death struggle with Napoleon, your President sticks in the cutlass in the hope of stealing Canada. He wants everything. But does it not occur to Mr Madison and all you bloody Yankees that if Napoleon should conquer Britain, he would not rest until he had retaken Canada. And how long would it be, Mr Adams, before the grand French armies marched into your precious States of America? Answer me that, eh?"

"I'm a mariner, not a politician."

"Was a mariner."

"That's right – was. And I was bringing a cargo of fine Virginia tobacco to Bristol for gentlemen like yourself who take snuff."

Cotgrave smiled a pleasant smile with his thick lips. "That goes in your favour, Mr Adams. In which case I shall cancel your execution."

"Thank you!" John never had any fear that the blustering old man would carry out his threat. "I'm just a prisoner of war, then," he said smiling.

"Prisoner of war! Good God, whatever gave you that idea? You're not a prisoner, nor are any of that scum out there in the prison yards. We're the prisoners, Mr Adams. Those two uniforms full of shit standing next to you are the prisoners. All the guards at this prison have been sent here as punishment for various misdemeanours. Now this man," he said, shaking one of the soldiers. "Rape or dirty boots – take your pick. Probably both." He shook the other soldier. "And this miserable bag of offal who can hardly stand on his feet – probably shitting himself on parade. It doesn't matter. And the French? Yes of course they're prisoners, for we and the French are natural enemies, since it's the way God wants it. Even so, they're well treated here in Dartmoor Prison. They have their own businesses, their own coffee-houses, even their own servants – and they gamble away fortunes on a game called faro. And the local people hold a market in their compound every day where the French can buy luxuries like food. Do you know, Mr Adams, what is engraved above the entrance to the prison?"

"Parcere Subjectis," answered John. "Virgil's charge to the people of Rome. 'Spare the vanquished'."

"And believe me, King George spares the vanquished from the bottom of his big fat heart. He has a soft spot for the Yankees, even though they mutinied against him. Some say he's insane." Cotgrave poured out two tankards of wine from a barrel and offered John one. "Take a drink, Mr Adams."

John took the tankard, not out of courtesy but necessity. He had been trussed up like a turkey cock at Exeter, thrown into the back of a cart, and rumbled and rattled over the cart-tracks of the moor. His escorts had stopped at Widecombe for ale, but he had been offered no refreshment. He was parched, and his tongue was rough and dry. He drained his tankard, and thirst compelled him to hold his mug out for more.

"Far too sparing is King George," went on Cotgrave. "Every man jack Yankee is free to walk out through the prison gate at any time. All he has to do is sign up for the British Navy and fight for the land of his forefathers. Just one voyage, one pleasant cruise on board one of His Majesty's ships and, if he wishes, he can return to Dartmoor Prison after the voyage; and King George has promised that any prize-money will be forwarded to him at this address. You see, when all is said and done, you're just twisted Englishmen who are being given the opportunity to straighten out. Look upon this establishment as a recruiting depot, and while you're trying to make up your minds, King George will pay you from his own pocket the sum of one shilling and six pence a day, which is more than these sloppy redcoats are getting. 'Parcere Subjectis,' eh? Oh, indeed, yes – too sparing if you ask me. Why, if you Englishmen-removed want more money, you've got your own agent, a Mr Beasley, to negotiate for you.''

''It's up to each man to follow his conscience,'' said John.

''Of course it is,'' smiled Cotgrave, replenishing John's tankard. ''Honour is the thing, isn't it? You are, I suppose, classed as an American officer?''

''I guess so.''

''No problem. No problem whatsoever. All you have to do is give me your word of honour and you can join your fellow parole officers in Ashburton, which is fast becoming an American township, or you can live with relatives in this country. You must have family connections in Britain – all Americans have. Again'' – Cotgrave stroked his stubbly chin and walked round John in examination – ''Yes, again the King will give you his commission in his navy – you'll have your own ship in no time. Why, one of your countrymen is an admiral who fought with Nelson at Trafalgar, and he's in line for a knighthood. We British are too forgiving at times. Naughty children can always come back to the family.''

Cotgrave tipped a mound of snuff on to the back of his hand and breathed it in. There was so much snuff in the air that John and the two soldiers sneezed, but the old man merely patted his chest as though he had taken in a breath of fresh country air. ''However,'' he went on, ''sometimes children can be very naughty, and you've been very naughty, haven't you, Mr Adams?''

''It was my duty to escape.''

''Of course it was. But when you were arrested outside God's cathedral at Exeter, you were wearing fancy French clothes, weren't you? A beautiful velvet jacket, if I may say so.'' He walked around John again and sniffed at him. ''And you're so clean and healthy and well fed. Somebody has been taking very good care of you, Mr Adams, and it hasn't been anybody from the townships, for we have a squad of soldiers in all those places. So it must have been somebody from the moorland, somebody in a secret place; the same somebody who has been supplying French officers with horses and passages in ships. You must remember, Mr Adams, that when a French officer escapes, he returns to France in order to kill more Englishmen. There is a French agent somewhere on Dartmoor, and you know who that agent is, and you could, if you wished, take us to the very spot from which that agent operates, and thus save the lives of Englishmen, the men who share the same English blood as yourself. Parole? We'll give you more than parole – we'll give you your unconditional freedom. Now than, what do you say, eh?''

John was in two minds. Sally had betrayed him. She had lied to him and cheated him; had taken him to the very threshold of freedom where he could almost smell the grass of New England, and then, with a kiss like a female Judas, a vicious Delilah, had turned him over to the muskets of the British.

Captain Cotgrave continued: ''A woman, a girl, a slut, a whore, a Doll Tearsheet, a Moll Flanders! Yes, me lad, we want her. We call her the Dartmoor Vixen. Come now, lead us to her, and we'll give you back your ship. How's that? And ye can sail away into the sunset, eh? Lead us to her.''

John gripped his fists so tightly that his knuckles and fingernails hurt. Yes, yes, he thought. But she would be hanged. Was that worth his ship or his freedom? He saw her face, he thought of the dollymin. He still loved her, although he hated her at the same time.

''I'll think about it,'' he replied.

''Of course you'll think about it, because you're a thinking man. And just to give you privacy in which to think, I shall confine you to the lock-up, the black hole, the *cachot*. And there you'll stay without food and in the dark until you think the right thoughts. I'm only doing my duty as an English officer, Mr Adams.''

''If I remember Bunyan correctly,'' answered John, ''Giant Despair flung Christian and his friend Hopeful into a black dungeon without food or drink. He cudgelled them and showed them the skulls of former victims. Blow me down, Captain

Cotgrave, if Christian didn't discover that he'd got the key to freedom in his possession all the time.''

"Lock him up!" ordered Cotgrave.

At the side of each large prison block was a small *cachot*, so-called by the French. They were built of thick, heavy rocks of granite, and they had domes of granite. There were no window spaces, just small holes for air, sometimes frosty air and misty air, to get through. They were always dark and damp, they were tombs for men who went into them half living and came out three-quarters dead. All the tall prison blocks were only six years old, having been built for French prisoners, they sparkled fresh granite grey. The *cachots* had been daubed with red paint, and the prisoners had painted skulls and skeletons on them.

When John was thrown into the cell, and the thick door was slammed and bolted, it was as though he had been struck blind. He lay on the earthen floor for several minutes blinking until he saw the tiny air-holes; they were not big enough to get a hand through, so that prisoners could not beg. There was an overpowering sweet smell of excreta from past prisoners, and there was a continuous buzz-buzz from bluebottles and wasps which had crawled through the holes and were more concerned with the excreta than with the human being, although one or two crawled on his face.

In a way, he was content to have been chucked into solitary confinement; he didn't want to hear stupid chatter about nothing. He had just been torn away from magic, some kind of sweet sorcery. He had been with Sally through the sunny summer months, when there had been no time, only sun-ups and sundowns which had passed quickly like the racing shadow of a small white cloud. There had been love-making and warm sunshine, foxes yelping, meadow larks singing high up, and blue moonlight lighting up the tors and animating their shapes. He had danced with Sally in this moonlight, twirling her around until her feet left the ground and they both became dizzy and fell in the heather; they had galloped swift horses and had toppled from them into a fast river; there had been the wonderful sense of freedom from knowing there were no people to see them; Dartmoor had been their Eden.

26

And then she had betrayed him. He banged his fist against the wall until it bled. She had turned him over to the redcoats on the very steps of a cathedral. He shoved his fist in his mouth to prevent himself shouting out that he hated her. But he didn't hate her, he loved her, and he blubbered like a baby because he did so. He had the power to betray her. He didn't know the exact location of her valley, but he knew it was to the east, and he could describe the tor near her home, and sufficient soldiers could comb the area and catch her. And she would hang. There would be laughter and singing, and jugglers and fire-eaters, and every man jack would ogle her as she danced from the rope. But he wouldn't let that happen; he would gallop to the scaffold and cut the rope with a sword, and he alone would defy the entire British Army. And he would hold her and kiss her, and sail on the *Boston Trader* to New England with her.

He lay unmoving for many hours. A night must have passed, for the pin-holes disappeared into blackness and the insects stopped buzzing. Perhaps he slept; it was hard for him to tell where his thoughts became dreams, or where his dreams became nightmares.

There were long periods of complete blackness, and periods of slightly grey; and in some of these periods John was brought bread and water. The cold had ceased to bother him, as did the flies and wasps and the smell of the lock-up. He was just a living thing. During one grey period he heard shouting, yelling and singing of the daily market. Outsiders were allowed to come inside the prison walls and set up their stalls and sell their wares, but only the eight thousand Frenchmen were allowed to go to the market; the two thousand Yankees had to buy their vegetables and pies to augment their prison rations at twice the price. This was because Captain Cotgrave considered the French to be respectable enemies; the Yankees were mutineers and should consider themselves lucky they were not hanging from yard-arms or being crow-picked in gibbets.

There had been other market days during John's black incarceration, but there was something about this noise and clatter that made him dimly aware. It was the singing of a sweet female voice.

"When seven long years did pass away,
 She put on mean attire,
 And she set off to London Town,
 About him to enquire,
 And as she passed along the highway,
 The weather being hot and dry,
 She sat her down on a green bank,
 And her true true love came riding by.''

It was Sally singing the ballad. It was definitely Sally. He knew her voice; she had sung many a time. She was a creature of song.

He felt that he was shut up in his coffin under the earth and hearing the flowers growing and the birds singing.

"O stay, O stay, thou goodly youth,
 She standeth by thy side,
 She is alive, she is not dead,
 But ready for to be thy bride.''

There was no doubt that it was Sally's voice, but it started a red hell of torture in his mind. Had she come to taunt him? Had she come to make communication with some French prisoner? He could not believe she had come merely to tell him she loved him. A woman who turned a man over to a line of muskets had hate and spite in her heart, if she had a heart at all. This truly was Doubting Castle ruled by Giant Despair. He resolved he would keep alive in order to confront her face to face.

At the beginning of the next dull grey period, which meant morning, there was one big noisy hullabaloo outside. This couldn't be the market; it was ten times noisier than the market. There were musket-cracks and orders of command. A deafening thud-thud-thud shook the door of his cell, making him afraid the thick rocks were going to fall in on him and bury him alive. It was as though cannon-balls were being aimed at the door. The door split and splintered from its bolts and hinges, and for a second everything was blinding white with daylight so that his eyes hurt. A huge Negro bent down to look in his cell. It could have been Satan. The man must have been over six feet in height, and he

28

was as bulky as an ox. On his head was a badgerskin cap: the tail hung down over one ear, while hanging from the other ear was a large earring. His face had been painted with red and yellow lines like a Mohawk. There was a string of horse shoes round his neck, and across his chest was tattooed in very large letters ANGEL GABRIEL. He carried a thick club about a yard long, which he tossed from hand to hand in rhythm; he also spoke in rhyme.

"I is Big Dick, and I is bigger dan all udder feller in de land o' da nigger. Dis Big Dick, and dis ma stick, break white man's head, make him go sick."

He rolled his eyes like a pendulum in co-ordination with his stick and his speech. Then he stopped rhyming and probed in the dark lock-up with his club.

"Yar suh, every day I talks in person to da Archangel of Gabriel, and dat archangel am sure de most gabrielest of all de archangels, ain't no lie. And he tells Big Dick dat foh certain dis great Dart-of-de-moor Dungeon an a-gonna sink under de deep blue sea in forty day and forty night. So hurry up outa dat black cage afore you becomes a fish."

Once again he began tossing his club to and fro from hand to hand, and rolling his eyes.

"Me daddy was a lion from de land o' Zion and me mam a crocodile from de bank o' de Nile. Come out dat cell so me can see if you is white or black like me. White man Yankee go to war, he say today is July Four."

John staggered out and ran; he wasn't too sure whether or not Big Dick would club him when he saw he was a white man.

The scene was like a macabre painting by Hieronymus Bosch. Thousands of men were fighting each other; many were on the ground bleeding; some seemed to be suspended upside-down. Yellow jackets fought yellow jackets, some Yankee yellow jackets had muskets, some French yellow jackets were waving swords. The superior numbers of the French seemed to be stopping the Yankees from moving towards the main gate. On the walls, redcoats were firing their muskets into the sky. John stooped down to ask a wounded man what it was all about.

"July the Fourth," said the man.

"I've been told," said John. "But why the commotion?"

29

"We got two Stars and Stripes. One has been captured and ripped to shreds by British bayonets. But we still got the other, and we want to hoist it above the main gate. But them Frenchies is stopping us." The man pointed. "Look behind you!"

The warning was too late. A redcoat came behind John and thudded him on the head with the butt of his musket.

"Get on your feet, Mr Adams. And drink this rum."

Captain Cotgrave stood over him with a tankard in his hand. John's head was painful, it hurt him just to move it, but he crawled to his feet, grabbed the tankard and gulped the rum.

"I invited you here because I need your help."

"Invited?" asked John, rubbing his sore head. "Was that it – invited?"

"You must forgive the British soldier. He's an ignorant sod, not too well schooled in the airs and graces of social pleasantries, I'm sorry to say. Now, Mr Adams, look out of the window and tell me what it's all about down there, if you please. Drink your rum, lad; there's more."

John looked down on the prison yards; it was more ghastly than it had seemed when he'd been down there amongst it. About eight thousand men were fighting each other, with several hundred Negroes leaning against the walls of the prison blocks and showing their white teeth with laughter at the spectacle. There were huge banners draped across the prison buildings. On one was emblazoned *Sailors Rights and Free Trade*, and on the other *Canada – or Dartmoor for Ever*. There were banners across the French blocks proclaiming *Liberté, Egalité, Fraternité* and *Vive Napoléon!* John was surprised about the Yankee muskets.

Cotgrave read his mind: "I think they buy them off the redcoats. Some of them would sell their own mothers for sixpence, but I think the going rate for a loaded musket is one shilling. You'll notice, Mr Adams, that I've ordered the garrison to shoot up in the sky."

"Very considerate of you."

"Indeed, yes, I've given the matter much consideration. I don't mind the Yankees killing a few Frenchmen – it means more

30

rations to go round. But I don't want my soldiers harming the Yankees. King George, God save him, wants them for his navy – and a Yankee without a hand ain't no use at loading cannons and firing broadsides. Now, sir, what's all this merry dance about?''

"It's Independence Day.''

"I know that better than you. I was there.''

"And the Americans want to fly their flag from the main gate alongside yours.''

"So what do I do? Order my garrison to shoot them up their arses?''

"Let them fly their flag. You've got two poles above the gate. Let the two flags fly side by side – it'll give a touch of colour to the place.''

"God, Mr Adams, the story of my naval career has been watching that bloody flag of yours going up a pole. What would King George say?''

"I thought he and you wanted us to be a family again, captain. Surely you want us to be friends so that the Americans down there will gladly volunteer for the King's Navy? Wouldn't it be a friendly gesture to fly the American flag?''

"And it'd end up with me being shot on a quarterdeck.''

The captain took a pinch of snuff, at the same time scattering enough tobacco powder to make John and his guard sneeze. "Clears the brain,'' said Cotgrave. "Come to think of it, Mr Adams, you could be right. A friendly gesture could get me a hundred recruits.''

"Two hundred,'' said John.

"A thousand even.''

"And a knighthood.''

"Yes, by George! You may be right.''

"Rule Britannia, if I may say so, captain.''

"I don't know about that. It's me pension I'm concerned about.''

The captain put his head through the door and called for a sergeant. Orders were given for the cannons to point outside the prison and discharge simultaneously to create a loud bang and get the attention of the rioters.

"Why not fire over their heads?'' asked John.

"Because you don't know these bloody soldiers. If I ordered them to fire over their heads, then some of your Yankees would lose their arses. They killed more Spaniards than Frenchmen in the Peninsula. That's why they're here. This way they may kill a few rabbits."

He then gave further orders that the Americans should be allowed to hoist their flag, and if the Frenchmen wouldn't stand and make way for them, the soldiers would shoot into them.

Both men went out on to the wall to watch. Within ten minutes there was a booming, crashing explosion from the cannons and all actions stopped in the yards. There was silence, and an announcement was made. The Frenchmen cleared a passage, and four Americans marched to the gate. The flag of the United States of America was raised over Dartmoor Prison. There was cheering and singing:

> "Yankee Doodle, keep it up,
> Yankee Doodle dandy;
> Mind the music and the step,
> And with the girls be handy."

A number of redcoats joined in, and some Yankees and British did a sort of jig out of relief. The French began to sing 'La Marseillaise', but on realising the Yankee song was about girls and dancing and was not a call to arms, sang instead:

> "Pour moi ne chante guère
> Car j'en ai un joli
> Dites-nous donc la belle
> Ou donc est votre mari?
> Auprès de ma blonde
> Qu'il fait bon, fait bon, fait bon
> Auprès de ma blonde, qu'il fait bon dormir."

What had started as carnage ended as carnival. The thousands of men laughed and sang and danced and whooped like Red Indians. Captain Cotgrave burst out laughing, and his laughter grew into the roar of an avalanche. He put his arm round John and drew him back to the table for more rum.

"By George, I took you for a man of logic from the start. And that you are, Mr Adams, that you are."

His laughter continued until tears streamed down his cheeks. He took more snuff, and John turned his head away so that he wouldn't sniff up any of the tobacco.

"And now I'll tell you a secret," went on the captain. "This very morning I sent a despatch to Plymouth with the resignation of my commission. It should be ratified in a few months. I just hope I get the thousand volunteers and my knighthood before then. It'll add to my pension." He sighed and wiped the tears from his face, leaving brown snuff streaks down his cheeks. "My last command, eh? And damn glad I am to be rid of it. I commanded a ship of the line under Nelson. I'm not a prison turnkey – by God, no! Just look at it out there! Ten thousand men going wild in some devil's barn dance." He prodded John, and began laughing again. "And d'y'know what decided me on resigning, eh? D'y'know what? Because yesterday I received a despatch ordering me to take command of the penal colony at Botany Bay! Botany Bay! By God, it may be Australia, but stack me if there wouldn't be a Stars and Stripes up a pole in next to no time with me in command."

John burst out laughing at the thought.

"College graduate, aren't you?" asked Cotgrave.

John nodded.

"I suppose they taught you to read and write?"

"Simple words."

"Then I've got a simple job for you, Mr Adams. During the few months left, I want you to be my adjutant."

"Adjutant?"

"I think my official adjutant deserted a few weeks ago, or else had his throat cut. Anyway, I haven't seen him since. You're a mariner, Mr Adams, and an educated man, and so am I. The guards are all soldiers, and they have their own officers who hide away, or maybe they've had their throats cut too. There, me lad, unofficial acting, unpaid adjutant, what?"

"I won't accept the King's commission."

"Nobody's offering it to you. Unless you take the oath of

33

allegiance, and I can't see you doing that in a hurry."

"I might swear an affidavit not to leave Dartmoor, and so accept parole."

"You'd have to live within the walls so as to be at hand."

"Fine. I'll live in the cell block with my countrymen. Just so long as I can go into Ashburton or Tavistock without let or hindrance from time to time."

"I shall write out the authority."

The captain held his hand out, which John took.

"All we need is a Bible to take your oath on," said Cotgrave. "Trouble is, finding a Bible. People throw them away when they set foot on the moor."

"Let the handshake suffice," said John. "However, there is some unfinished business between us."

The captain raised his eyebrows.

"The person you refer to as the Darmoor Vixen, if she exists," explained John

"Oh, she exists – as you well know, to your cost. Don't worry, I've sent a squad of trackers out with orders not to return unless she's their prisoner. We'll see her petticoats fluttering in the breeze yet, Mr Adams."

The momentary picture of Sally being hanged sickened John. He must get to her before the redcoats.

The first thing John Adams had done upon arriving at Dartmoor War Prison from the prison ship *Hector*, lying off Plymouth, was to escape. Consequently he had not the remotest idea how his Yankee compatriots lived, or existed. They were allocated six prison blocks, each four storeys high; each floor like a barren stable except for the stout wooden posts on which were slung hammocks, one above the other, for the prisoners. At the end of each room was a large copper cauldron, under which a fire was kept alight night and day for warmth and for cooking. The men tossed their rations into the cauldron, and shared out the stew and the soup in their wooden bowls.

Many of the men were half naked, having lost their blankets and clothing to the French on the faro tables. One block was set aside for dangerous prisoners; these were usually Yankees who had injured or murdered their fellow-prisoners. When found guilty by a prisoners' court, they were branded with an M on their cheeks.

What appalled John more than the physical condition of the men was their mental state. All spirit had left them; they were beaten and degraded. They were just living creatures shuffling around, without a spark of humour in any one of them; their guards were more criminal than they. To add to their misery and fear, they were hounded by a renegade gang of their own countrymen who called themselves the 'Rough Alleys'. If a man dared win a few shillings on the faro game, the 'Rough Alleys' threatened to slit his throat unless he handed over a half.

The French were allowed the daily run of the market, from which the Yankees were barred. Consequently they had to buy from the French, who usually auctioned the food off to the highest bidders. This meant that the faro table was always a temptation to hungry men who hoped to win enough for food. The French were also permitted to run coffee-houses and eating-rooms; this again was forbidden to the Yankees.

Always facing the miserable prisoners was the banner over Captain Cotgrave's office – *Come Yankees One and All! Join the King's Navy! Good Food, Good Prize-Money, and Freedom!'*

John Adams was overwhelmed by the prisoners' obstinate patriotism, which they took to the point of starvation. They could at any time accept the offer to be well fed and decently clothed in the British Navy. Dartmoor would be a name in the early history of his country to rank with Concord, Lexington and the Battle of Bunker Hill. He resolved that all men would give their name followed by their town; it would give them some small pride. He tried it on himself – John Adams of Boston, Massachusetts – and he found himself walking with a stride. He now had two loves and two loyalties – one to his countrymen, the other to Sally. At the same time, he had a begrudging regard for his head gaoler, Captain Cotgrave. For the sake of both, he now had to become a good adjutant, as Cotgrave termed it.

"Dartmoor is a magic place," said Cotgrave.

The use of the word magic in Captain Cotgrave's vocabulary startled John, who had been thinking of Sally's cottage as some kind of magic.

"Yes, absolute magic," went on Cotgrave. "Or at least for eight thousand Frenchmen, mmm? The Corsican promised his soldiers untold wealth, but he didn't say they'd have to come to Dartmoor to get it. Would you believe, Mr Adams, that in the few years they've been here, they've counterfeited twenty thousand pounds in perfect shillings. Perfect, beautiful, shiny shillings! I don't know how they do it! There is King George's head perfectly guillotined on every one! They are very rich Frenchmen, and they will go home to buy themselves châteaux and vineyards. They scatter their money on the daily markets, they buy things I can't afford to buy. And the trades people no longer rumble their carts from Tavistock and Moreton; they've built homes around the prison, where they live and keep their supplies. A town is being built – Princetown; ugh, I'd call it Napoleonville! And all on counterfeit shillings!"

He opened the fat, thick safe in the corner; it was packed with bags of coins. "That's just a little of the money we've caught them with. By God, I could live like a lord!"

John noticed Cotgrave put the key back in a desk drawer. He took the opportunity to talk him into allowing the Yankees access to the market.

At first, the captain wouldn't hear of it.

"Egad, Mr Adams, and spoil them? If your Yankees started to live in the luxury of the French, they'd never even think of joining the King's Navy. Would you? I wouldn't."

"My Yankees are broken. They honestly don't care whether they live or die. They're so dispirited, they no longer desire freedom. But if you allowed them just a taste of freedom, so that they remembered what it was, they'd come back to life, and want to clear away from the prison. How best? Not walking circles on the moor until they dropped dead, but marching out through the gate to sign up on your ships to the wide, open sea."

"By George, sir! What was the name of your college?"

"Harvard."

"I take my hat off to Harvard. They taught you logic – or if they didn't teach you logic, they taught you persuasive rhetoric." Cotgrave burst out laughing, sniffed up an ounce of snuff, banged his tankard on the table for John to refill. "All right, your bloody Yankees can go to market, but, dammit, what they can buy with their allowance will be precious little."

"They might be able to use persuasive rhetoric."

"You will, of course, superintend the market."

John was delighted, but he was never quite sure whether Cotgrave was trying to trap him; he was aware that the Englishman was a wily old dog. Perhaps he'd shown him the money as a temptation. Maybe he hoped John would lead him to Sally by giving him enough rope. He decided, to hell with it, he would walk eyes open into the first trap, and he helped himself to a bag of coins.

That night, when the only inside light was from the cauldron fires, he let shillings drop at random. Altogether he disposed of a hundred pounds. At least some lucky Yankees would have money for the market.

The next day, the yard filled up with traders, and the Frenchmen and Yankees rushed from their blocks. There was some scuffling and fighting at first. The French were angered at the Yankees being allowed to the market, and blows were struck when the Yankees bought their own vegetables; but Cotgrave backed up his concession by ordering a squad of redcoats to fire a volley over their heads, whereupon things settled down.

John was amused to notice, and how he wished Captain Cotgrave could witness, that 'persuasive rhetoric' was not necessarily the prerogative of Harvard graduates. Whereas the French tried to beat the traders down by denigrating their produce – "Cabbage, you call it, yes? We would not feed our pigs with it in France" – the Yankees sweet-talked them – "What a very fine cabbage. I wish we could grow them like that in America" – and of course the cabbage went for the cheapest price to the American. "Such nice gentlemen" was the general opinion. John watched with satisfaction.

A Jew with a black beard down below his chest shouted out that he had the finest clothing in England for sale; all had been worn by dukes and earls.

Big Dick approached the Jew's stall. With Big Dick was another Negro, a man less than five feet. Big Dick swung his club.

37

"Is you a child of Israel, what build de pyramid in de sand, and follow Moses to de promised land?"

"I'm of the Hebrew faith, sir."

"Is it true what I supposes, dat you is de son of Emperor Moses?"

"No, sir, I do not have that honour."

"Den listen here, if you ain't de son of Emperor Moses, all of ma business here now closes. Big Dick's ma name, and a saint by trade, and I only does business wid de same brigade."

"Yes, yes, sure, sure," said the Jew. "I am the son of Father Moses." The old man turned away, looked up at the sky, and shrugged. "Forgive me, Lord, for taking his name in vain, but business is business."

"I tell you make me one big coat what stretch from de ankle up to ma throat. It gotta be wool, and it gotta be green, same like de pasture where David been."

"Green wool, yes, sure, sure," said the Jew, and he stood on a box to take the giant's measurements.

Big Dick drew his companion towards him with his club. "Dis here assistant Deacon John. Him want top hat for his head fit on. Eighteen inches high, no less, no more. Same kinda hat what Jacob wore."

Big Dick flung some shillings down on the stall as a deposit, and the Jew rubbed his hands with happiness.

All the traders were happy, happier than they'd ever been, for now they were dealing with people who spoke the same language. It became a busy, friendly market, and John, like the Jew, rubbed his hands with contentment. There was a good deal of noise, but above the noise he heard Sally singing:

> " 'O mother, mother make my bed,
> O make it soft and narrow:
> My love has died for me today,
> I'll die for him tomorrow.'
>
> 'Farewell,' she said, 'Ye virgins all,
> And shun the fault I fell in:
> Henceforth take warning by the fall
> Of cruel Barbara Allen.' "

38

He made his way indirectly towards her, but shaking hands with the men and kissing the women on the cheeks as he did so, and always chatting to every trader, until he finally arrived at Sally's stall, where she was selling jams.

"I don't know whether I should talk to you," he began. "I could have died for you, true enough."

"And I'm prepared to die for you tomorrow," she said. "Go on, turn me over, as I did you."

"Why did you do it?"

"Because I wanted to keep you like a thrush in a cage. You would have escaped to America, and I could not come with you. I would never have seen you again. Please believe me, John, I did it out of love for you."

"I've accepted parole. When can I come and see you?"

"Always."

"How do I get there? I'd never find your valley."

"You'll get a horse from Lady Hen. She's the next one you've got to kiss." Sally laughed. "Quite a ladies' man, going the rounds."

"I can't differentiate. Captain Cotgrave's watching me through his telescope. They're after you."

"They'll never find me. The moor will get them first."

"It might get me first, even on horseback."

"Not if you follow the tors. There's Fox and Devil and Secret and Hound and Skull. Can you remember?"

"As if my life depended upon it." He kissed her on the cheek, and moved towards Lady Hen, a fat lady who was the shape of the eggs she sold. "I shall be calling on you for a horse, one of these days," he told her.

"Is that all?"

After a bit more chin-wagging with John, Sally gathered him in her arms and gave him a long kiss on the lips. She went on laughing as John moved on to the man who was selling pig pies.

The commandant still had him in his ship's telescope.

CHAPTER THREE

Picture of Horrible Devourers

THE English sergeant, who had been in charge of the party that had been sent to track down the Vixen of Dartmoor, had been found dead on the moor. He had died in a grotesque manner. The knee of one leg was bent, as though he'd been running, while the other leg was bent backwards, as though he'd been kneeling. One arm was pointing towards the sky, the other was stretched sideways. In that position he had died and stiffened. But his face was more frightening than the contortions of his body. One eye had been pecked away, no doubt by the ravens; but the other eye was wide open and protruding and had a red ring round the staring eyeball. His nostrils were extended as though he had made a great fight; and his mouth was wide open, and although silent, it screamed. Captain Cotgrave had ordered the body to be displayed in the prison yard. It had been carried in and tied to a chair for all to see.

"Let 'em see the horrors that await them on the moor. It'll deter both the soldiers and their prisoners from deserting or escaping better than a thousand bayonets. Fear, Mr Adams, fear – the great deterrent, eh? Don't worry, he'll be given a decent burial after he's fulfilled his purposes."

"It's inhuman."

"What is?"

"Displaying him."

"It's not my act which is inhuman; indeed, I'm very human in showing the men under my command and charge what inhuman forces are out there. You can't tell me that man's death was by natural causes, Mr Logician?"

The Frenchmen and the Yankees gathered round the body and

stared. They didn't want to view the grisly corpse, but something inside each man compelled him to look at it and burn it on his memory.

"The man who thought up this prison on the moor was called Tyrewhit. If you ask me, it should have been Firewhit, for it's the work of the devil."

"Sinners in the hands of an angry God," said John softly.

"Stick to your Puritan thoughts," grumbled Cotgrave. "But I'll blame it on the good old-fashioned devil, like the joker on a playing-card. It's evil."

"You once called it magic."

"Evil magic, sorcery to turn a man's brain! There was another man with him; he was found with his head in the river – the rest may have been eaten by a devourer. There are no wounds on his body, there was food in pouch. Did you see his eye? It was full of fear. Did you see his mouth? He was screaming, and I can hear that scream going through me, and so can you. There never was such fear."

"Amen to that!"

"And d'y'know, Mr Adams, that man's death could have been avoided if you had given me the name and location of the French agent. I observed you in the market, but you kissed all the women."

"With the girls being handy," said John.

"Whatever," said Cotgrave. "Look on that man, and bear in mind that your obstinacy brought about his death through fear. Need some rum, Mr Adams?"

The sight of the twisted dead man became a mental plague amongst the Yankees. John listened to their talk.

"We was taken to Saginaw, and we was guarded by them Huron Indians, and fiends they was at that, waving their tomahawks at us, and whooping and dancing. We was expecting to have the scalps torn from our heads any time o' the night and day. 'Tis said as how they skin some Yankee boys alive so cleverly that they can see their own skins being nailed to a tree, and 'tis said as how they hang other Yankee boys upside-down over a slow fire to cook their brains while they're still thinking with them. But if y'ask me, I'd as soon take my chances with them Hurons as step

41

out in that devil's garden out there.''

"I heard tell as how Satan drives a pack o' red-eyed wolf-dogs round the moor like a whirlwind, and they devour a man's soul but spit out his body. I reckon that man out there had his soul eaten.''

"'Tis said a man can be riding a horse, and a pair of hairy hands, just hands on their own, takes the reins and gallops him into hell, alive – alive and kicking, and screaming and crying and shitting himself.''

From a corner of the block a man burst out crying. His sobs were like those of a woman: "I want to go home! Please let me go home!'' The man was John Taylor of New York. He had been one of the militia prisoners shipped across from Canada. He married just before entering the militia, and men found him tedious with his everlasting talk of his bride Susan. Taylor had shown an interest in painting, and John Adams had placed an order with the Jew for some paints, oils and brushes. A sized canvas had been supplied by one of the redcoats from the ammunition store. Taylor had become far too busy painting Susan to talk about her, and the painting was shaping up well. She was turning into a lovely woman, and most of the prisoners were interested in Susan's progress; many fell in love with her image, and some asked Taylor to paint her in the nude. But the talk went back to the terrors of Dartmoor.

"'Tis said as how there was a woman who poisoned five husbands, and when she died she turned into a black dog and runs the moor looking for throats to tear open.''

"I heard as how there's a stage-coach full o' skeletons, and driven by a rider without a head on his shoulders.''

"D'y'think them skeletons could have been the five husbands what was poisoned?''

"How the hell should I know?''

"No, but it's an interesting point, you must admit.''

John had heard enough. The men were grouping together round the cauldron, and touching each other for safety.

"Oh, for heaven's sake ease up! You're like children afraid of the dark for fear of the bogy man. I was lost on the moor for many nights and never once saw a ghost. All I saw were birds and beasts,

42

who were more afraid of me than ever I was of them. There's no danger on the moor. It's the living you've got to be on your guard against," he shouted.

He may have convinced others, but he had not totally convinced himself. A fear of an unknown danger lurked somewhere in his soul, and a fear for Sally most of all. Maybe what was out there had been awakened, like some prehistoric monster that had slept for a thousand years; maybe the imagination had become flesh. He felt the need to protect Sally.

His words about guarding against the living came true sooner than he or anybody else expected. A man rushed into the block to gasp out that James Pickerton of Hampton, Virginia, had been found with his throat cut.

"'Twas them eight Rough Alleys what murdered him for sure, cos William Riley of Philadelphia saw the whole thing. 'Twas for a coupla shillings."

John had to examine his second gruesome body that day. He asked the redcoats to arrest the eight Rough Alleys and lock them up in *cachots*, and arranged for the body to be cleaned and prepared for burial. In the morning he reported the homicide to Captain Cotgrave.

"Very interesting!" said Cotgrave.

"Interesting? Is that all you can say? Very interesting?"

"What more can I say? Mr Pickerton is dead, and nothing can bring him back. But what do we do with your Rough Alleys? They're civilians and don't come within my scope. There's nothing in King's Regulations. I can't judge. Haven't you got your own method of dealing with homicides? Why bother me?"

He shrugged his shoulders.

"I think they should have a trial."

"D'y'think they're guilty?"

"Yes."

"Well, hang 'em!"

"I only think; I don't know. That's why I want a trial."

"Well, I'll tell you what to do. You ride on to the Justice of the Peace at Exeter, and tell them I'll be sending eight Americans for trial. They'll arrive by cart under escort in a week's time."

"Me?"

43

"You're on parole. I'll extend your parole to Exeter. Be on your way, Mr Adams."

A white stallion was placed at John's disposal and he was supplied with an army officer's old red coat. He showed his letter of authority at the main gate and rode down the lane into Princetown, straight to the Jew's house. The old man bowed him in and immediately began showing his collection of secondhand clothing.

"Now examine if you will this beautiful coat. Feel the material; it will last you a lifetime, oh a lifetime. I am a fool to part with such melodious garments. Worn by the Earl of Winchester, none other. Where do you come from?"

"Boston."

"Ah, Boston. It is the Earl or the Duke of Boston? No matter; this coat will be finer than anything he wears. Just a few stitches here and there and a little scrubbing, and the gold embroidery will shine in the dark."

"I just want a dirty old green or grey coat. Something the colour of the moorland," said John.

"Are you an escaped prisoner?"

"No – I'm on parole. But I want to blend in with the moor. I don't want to stand out like a sore finger."

The son of Moses handed John a dirty old jacket.

"This is old," John said. "Maybe there is a mouse in the pocket."

"Then I don't charge you for the mouse. It was worn by a farmer who came to the moor to grow potatoes, swedes, turnips – but all he dug up were rocks. He sold me his jacket to buy ale. So people will take you for a rock-grower."

"Good. That's what I am."

His next call was at the cottage of Lady Hen. She wasn't in, so he decided to wile away a little time at one of the township's two taverns. There was the Devil's Elbow and the Plume of Feathers. The Plume of Feathers was the noisiest, and it was Johns choice. He assumed it was easier to get lost in a crowd.

It was a soldiers' tavern. The ceiling, which was brown with tobacco, nearly touched a tall man's head; soldiers wearing bearskin caps had to remove them. The general cry was "Sit down!" The tobacco fog hurt John's eyes. He had to push towards the bar to get a tankard of ale.

"Who the bloody hell do you think you are?" snarled a redcoat, as John's pushing caused him to tip some beer into his face.

"I'm a rock-grower."

"That's different, mate. Here, nudge in!" The soldier made way for him. "Where you from, mate?"

"Boston," said John, without thinking, as readily as he had answered the Jew.

The soldier's eyes lit up.

Lincolnshire, eh? Same as me! I'm from Sleaford! Here I'll pay for that!" The soldier flung a sixpence on the counter to pay for John's drink. "A rock-grower from Lincolnshire, eh? I ain't never met a rock-grower before. I met a poacher or two, though." And he immediately burst into song, a melody which fortunately John had heard in New England:

"When I was bound apprentice, in famous Lincolnshire,
   Full well I serv'd my master for more than seven year,
   Till I took up to poaching, as you shall quickly hear;
   Oh, 'tis my delight on a shining night, in the season of the year."

John looked around as he sang and waved his tankard of brimming, frothy beer. There was elbow-wrestling at one table; two men made contorted faces as they strained to bring each other's arm down, with the crowd shouting: "Go on, spit in his bleeding eye!"

There was another gang in a corner taking part in a drinking bout. The object seemed to be gaining promotion by supping a tankard in one gulp: a private could become a corporal, and thence to a sergeant and so on. John doubted if any man could make general while still standing.

Other men were tossing coins; others playing cards. And in another corner John noticed three differently uniformed soldiers supping and laughing. He recognised them as William Brown of

45

the American ship *Argus*, Robert Murray of Newport, Rhode Island, and John Burns of North Carolina. He was proud and amused at their audacity.

After a time, soldiers began to spit on the floor, a man was sick, voices got louder, language became coarser and men threatened to fight each other. John guessed it was time to leave; he hoped Lady Hen was at home. It didn't take him more than a minute to find the cottage with the horseshoe on the wall, and the old egg woman came to the door. "I thought you was a customer," she said.

"I am."

"Not for eggs nor not for comfort."

"For a horse."

"You got a horse. That ain't no hen."

"It's a fine bright white stallion. And I want a grey horse, one that blends with the moor. They set me up on a white horse with a red coat on my back, an easy target for a man with a ship's telescope. The commandant has obviously sent a man to follow me, so I'll leave the white horse and the red coat here with you."

"I'll leave you to go to the stable. There's a dapple-grey mare just a-waiting for you. And there's another mare to keep your white horse company. All I want now is a big, burly sergeant, then we're all happy."

John rode onto the moorland with several hours in hand before it got dark. He had no intention of being alone on the moor at night. Fox, Devil, Secret, Hound and Skull ran through his brain. He reined up and looked around the tors; one had to look like a fox. No, he couldn't see one. He paced the horse a little further. Any tor could look like a fox; any tor could look like Lady Hen; any tor could look like Captain Cotgrave. His enthusiasm had run away with him; it was an impossible task; he was a Theseus in the labyrinth of the Minotaur, only there was no Ariadne to help him. He longed to be back at the Plume of Feathers singing 'The Lincolnshire Poacher'; he longed to be back in Cotgrave's office turning over the ledgers. The prison was still in sight; he could return. And then, of all the tors, he saw a collection of rocks that could look like a fox; at least it looked more like a fox than the others. He galloped towards it.

46

Horse and rider panted on the top of Fox Tor, and once more he had to scan the hilltops. This time he had more than a devil to look for, he had a tracker with a telescope. Yes, he saw movement and the glint of light in a lens, or he thought he did. Anyway, he could not afford to take chances; he must assume he was being observed and followed. His eye could make out, if he dimmed it by letting his eyelid part close, a collection of rocks in the distance which could represent two horns. Of course it did not have to represent the devil; it could be a tor on which some person back in history claimed he had seen the devil, or some tor at which people had gathered to worship or sacrifice to the devil. Yet he had to take a chance, and he galloped in a roundabout course towards it. By now he had lost sight of the prison and, looking back, the fox on Fox Tor looked like a fox. On closer inspection, the two horns no longer looked like the devil's horns. Perhaps this was another betrayal of Sally's; perhaps she intended him to get lost and die because he knew she was an agent. And yet Lady Hen had been confident he would meet up with Sally, for she had given him a message to give to her. "Tell yon wench, there are two to meet at the Chagford cock-fight a week come Saturday," she had said.

And now look around for a secret. How could a shape represent a secret? It could have been a place where lovers held a clandestine tryst. But it was there plain enough; there was a finger pointing to the sky as a person would indicate a secret to another, a sort of shush in stone. Sermons in stones, Shakespeare had said. He wished he had not thought of the Minotaur. It was a disadvantage to be clever when in the wilderness. Better to be primitive. He thought of the look of horror on the dead sergeant's face and wondered if he would meet such a horror. He turned and galloped to the Secret Tor.

And on Secret Tor it was impossible to determine Devil's Tor, or indeed which was the last tor he had left. It wasn't far from twilight, and the time of dreadful fear when he had to face his Minotaur. One tiny consolation was that his pursuer would be a hell of a sight more scared than he was, and without the advantage of a route. Yes, he was sure it was a route, and he cursed himself for having earlier misgivings about Sally.

47

Hound Tor was easy. It was a hound seated on its haunches, and looking to the sky as though baying to a moon.

"Oh, 'tis my delight on a shining night, in the season of the year," sang John. "My delight on a shining night."

One more to go, and he felt he could take an evasive detour through a gully which led him to the far side of Hound Tor. The sun was sinking fast behind the hills, but luckily he was heading east so that there was enough red sunset to light up the tors ahead of him, and he could see the skull as clearly as if it had belonged to a human. It grinned across the moorland. John rode straight at it. On the crest he was just able to discern Sally's cottage, but only because he was looking for it. A stranger's eye could have swept the valley and seen only rocks.

"In the season of the year," he sang, and raced the horse to Sally's cabin.

Sally's little stone cottage was lighted, if lighted it could be called, by one candle; even the fire was dark red and gloomy.

"Good!" she said as he walked in. "Now I can light the lantern and stir the fire. I never keep much light showing when I'm on my own." She lit the lantern, and then went over to John and put her arms round him. "And now tell me you love me," she commanded.

"I think it was Orpheus who went into Hades to recover his bride Eurydice. I've done the same sort of thing this evening – and if that isn't love, what is?"

"Yes, you've passed the test. You pass all the tests, my John. And now it's my turn to pass the test. You see if I don't cook you a meal fit for a king."

"King George?"

"Charles the Third, of course. Who would have been King of England."

"How about King John?"

"He'll do. Better than Orpheus. Somebody sold me a horse called Orpheus. Kiss me, King John!"

They ate until they could eat no more; they made love until they could make love no more. When at last they went out to breathe the sharp night air of the moor, the moon was balancing on a tor.

48

"That's Sally Tor," said John.

"So, you make yourself into a king, and me you turn to stone. Thank you!"

He gave her waist a gentle squeeze. "You'll be my queen," he whispered.

"Will I? I wonder," she said wistfully.

"There's one terrified Englishman out there," said John. "He followed me, but I threw him off the scent. The entire garrison is afraid of demons and devils, Sally. And I was afraid for you."

"Of me being eaten by a dragon?"

"The moor isn't real."

"The moor is very real. And harmless. Don't worry, John. There's nothing to worry about. I'll survive. As obviously you will. Did Lady Hen kiss you again?"

"No, but she gave me a message to give you. She said there's two to meet at the Chagford a week on Saturday."

"Two? That's me and you, then. Oh, say you'll come, John. You'll love Chagford. It's where a bride was shot dead at the altar the very minute she was wedded."

"And that's why I'll love it?"

"There's the cockfight."

"That's something I'd rather miss, thank you."

"Well, come to keep me company, then. There'll be French officers there."

"You win. You may be safe from demons and devils, but I wouldn't trust French officers."

"Then you'll come to protect me?"

"Let's not go."

"I must."

"Why?"

"The two are two French officers, and I've to take them horses, and arrange passage. I think I'll try Tor Quay this time. Yes, I should get a fishing-boat if the Frenchmen have the money. So you see, John darling, we've got to go to Chagford. Please?"

He told her he was on his way to Exeter to notify them of the imminent arrival of men accused of murder, and Sally said she would ride off the moor with him, then take the right road for Tor Quay. They set off at daybreak.

49

For a short time they walked their horses, and suddenly Sally called to him to look at something. Between two small rocks of granite in the ground a solitary forget-me-not was growing.

"Will you look at that, John? It's me. One lonely little flower growing between the rock in the wilderness, and it grows, and it will be here next year, and next year. Oh, yes, that's me. You could take that flower in its own soil, and transplant it in the ruins of Buckfast Abbey where the soil is rich, and the ghost of the monks should sing their 'Ave Marias' and 'Sancta sanctorum' over it. And it would die."

They parted where the road divided. John reined for Exeter and the magistrates; Sally tapped the flank of her horse for the fishing village of Tor Quay. John was a worried man. He loved Sally more than life itself, and yet he had given his word of parole. But then he had given his word to a man and a country his own country was at war with. But as long as he kept his word, he would be in a position to make life bearable for thousands of his fellow-prisoners. Surely, to accompany Sally on an escape arrangement would be a breach of parole. It would mean the *cachot*, and no further help for the prisoners, possibly the suspension of market concessions and the removal of their flag from the main gate. Even to know of the escape plan and say nothing about it, might be construed a breach of parole. But always he saw Sally's face.

John returned his horse and coat in exchange for his prison issue to Lady Hen on his return from Exeter. She was singing her hens a lullaby, and they were lined up with one eye open, the other eye shut, as though she had ordered them to form ranks.

" 'Cockadoodledoo! My dame has lost her shoe; my master's lost his fiddling-stick, and knows not what to do.' There, there me little ones, close your pretty eyes and dream o' chanticleer, then wake up refreshed and satisfied and lay a lot of big ha'penny eggs for them gentlefolk up in the Prince o' Wales castle." She addressed John. "Ah, me Yankee doodle lover boy, I see you've done your duty."

"My duty? What's my duty?" asked John with a question more directed to himself than Lady Hen.

50

"Why, to deliver my message, of course!"

"Yes, I delivered your message."

"We'll make a spy of you yet. You're a hero, a very hero!"

John needed a drink of ale before he returned through the gate. To call him a spy had been to call him a snake, and it left a bad taste in his mouth. He ordered a tankard at the Elbow and had to suffer a loud-mouthed redcoat, who wiped his mouth with the back of his hand and spat on the floor repeatedly.

"There was me entire platoon killed 'cept me," the redcoat boasted. "So at night I crept over the field and went through their pockets, and would ye know that from the whole platoon of them I only got the sum of two shillings and sixpence, I ask yer. I'da got more from the hedgehogs. And that from an English regiment what carried Salamanca. And while I was crawling about, me head knocked against another man's head what was doing the same. Could be a Frenchman, I thought, so I slit his throat according to the rules o' war. Turned out he was one of our'n, and he'd no but twopunce on him. War's cruel. Not worth getting hanged for taking from the dead. 'Tis preserving the image o' King George the Third, ain't it just? And what'd a worm do with a penny? Go looking for a whore worm, and saying I've got a penny for yer favours, me lady. No, it's such as me what keeps King George in circulation."

John looked at the fat King's face on the coin with which he paid for this mug of ale, and left for the prison. He looked up as he led his horse through the gate; the Stars and Stripes was still flying alongside the Union Jack.

Once inside the compound, he felt a warm security. The prison had its own kind of freedom – a freedom from too much freedom. As a small boy he had played truant from school on an urge to go fishing. He caught no fish and it started to rain, and the rain came down heavily. Lightning flashed across the river and the water jumped in a thousand mushroom plops. He ran into the forest, and he was lost; there was no sun to give him direction. Any moment he expected to meet an Indian with a scalping knife, or a bear with long claws, or a wild cat with great sharp teeth. A moose bellowed, and he ran desperately through the bramble bushes, tearing his legs, knees and hands, and he cried aloud for

51

help. Finally he reached a lane and found his way home, and the expected happened – his father sent him up to his bedroom and locked him in. He sat on an upright chair at the window and watched the rain outside, and he had never felt so secure. This was how he felt now.

Most of the men were half asleep in their hammocks, moaning and groaning and talking in their sleep. Taylor was painting his picture by lantern-light in the corner. John looked at the painting. It was good, very good. It was nearly finished, and the portrait was of a very beautiful woman. "She's a lovely lady," he told Taylor.

"Oh, she is," said Taylor. "And I still can't believe she consented to marry me. And she plays the clavichord. Not many can play the clavichord."

"I can't, for one. The clavichord, eh?"

"'Twas the family's – they brought it over. They were Cavaliers until Oliver Cromwell chopped the King's head off with an axe, and they came over to Virginia. But 'twas in New York I met her, and 'tis in New York we live. And she plays Johann Sebastian Bach."

"Johann Sebastian Bach, eh?"

"Course she plays the fine ballads as well. Oh yes, 'Barbara Allen' and 'Early One Morning' and even the songs of this new man Thomas Moore."

"Isn't that something, eh?" John patted Taylor on the shoulders. "A truly beautiful lady."

He had to get away from Susan's eyes; she was telling him something. She was telling him he could have married a charming lady like her once upon a time in Boston, and that he could have walked to church with her on Sundays, and raised his hat to neighbours; but the primeval Sally had spoiled him for ever for the grace and charm of fine ladies. He either had to get a thousand miles away from Sally's bewitching influence, or surrender to her charms. She had proved that she would not let him escape. He could free himself from his love for her only under escort to the music of the fife and drum. He would consider enlisting in the British Navy and encouraging as many men as he could to enlist with him. If some stayed on in prison, well the devil take the hindmost.

He reported to Captain Cotgrave.

"Ah, I see you accomplished your duty, Mr Adams. 'England expects,' what!"

Duty again. Damn duty – oh damn and blast duty! John thought.

Captain Cotgrave was bright and breezy after a weekend of chicken and champagne, smuggled of course, in Plymouth; and he shuffled papers noisily to prove it. The first caller was the American agent Mr Reuben Beasley, and Cotgrave tactfully left the office in order to give John privacy.

"The men need more money," John demanded.

"There isn't a chance."

"Oh yes there is."

"Look Mr Adams, explain to the men that things are going bad for our country. We've surrendered at Beaver Dam, and our losses are heavy at Niagara. Our ships are bottled up in port. Congress needs all the money it can get to sustain fighting forces for the protection of our United States, and they'll not allow one dollar or cent to keep prisoners in safety in England."

"Safety?"

"You're alive, aren't you?"

"Mr Beasley, there are well over three thousand Americans in Dartmoor Prison, and they look upon me as their leader. I am prepared to march them all down to Plymouth to take up service in the British Navy. Now, sir, what would Congress say to that? That would be a greater humiliation than Beaver Dam or Detroit or Niagara."

"Er. . . there could be a soap allowance, I suppose."

"And winter is coming on, Mr Beasley. They'll need woollen clothing and leather shoes. Snow is on the way."

"There could, I suppose, be a clothing allowance."

"And a coffee allowance. They'll need hot coffee to warm their cold bellies."

"I'll see what I can do."

"And we'll call it macaroni."

"Maca. . . Mr Adams. Oh, I see. Good day to you!"

"And good day to you too, sir!"

Bang went the British Navy idea! John realised that he had

bargained with Beasley and won – yet he had personally lost. He could no more march his men to Plymouth than fly over the walls of the prison. In accepting Beasley's offer for soap, clothing and coffee, he had committed himself to stay with the men. He supposed that helping a couple of French officers to escape now and then was neither here nor there, a small price for helping the Yankees and keeping things smooth at the prison; and he doubted whether British victories or losses would be affected one iota. What's more, he could still have his beloved Sally. Yes, she was his beloved Sally, and he loved her more than all the sophisticated Susans and their clavichords and their lasses with the delicate airs.

Captain Cotgrave burst in and, after making straight for the brandy jar, gulped down a mug of brandy.

"I don't know what I'm about to be visited by heaven help me, and this is good brandy, but I saw them coming. They're here!" He pointed to the door, as Big Dick and Deacon John came in. Big Dick was wearing a massive green overcoat which trailed on the floor and covered his feet, and Deacon John wore the tallest of stovepipe hats on his head.

"What d'y'want?" demanded the captain.

The reply from Deacon John surprised Cotgrave because he spoke in an impeccable English accent, in fact that of a true-blue aristocrat.

"Perhaps we should invite His Royal Highness and Sainthood to express himself in his own inimitable fashion, sir, with sincere respect and begging your pardon."

Deacon John noticed the snuffbox on the table and walked across to it. "A fascinating snuffbox, sir. Silver, by Jove! Of the style used in Versailles by the court of Louis the Sixteenth. Confound those. . . those Jacobin ruffians! May I?" He took a pinch of snuff, sniffed it gently up each nostril, and screwed up his eyes more with delight than irritation. "Superb quality, sir, if I may say so. The very choicest Virginia leaf, with perhaps a grain or two of rosemary. I am in debt to you, sir."

Captain Cotgrave, who had turned to stone throughout this performance, exploded: "Good God! are you trying to ape an Englishman? I'll have you in the *cachot*!"

"Good gracious me, no, sir. I am an Englishman born and bred. I was formerly head manservant to His Grace the Duke of Kent – but, alas, he lost me in a card game to a rough Virginian planter. Hearts when he should have played diamonds – you know how it is. I ended up picking tobacco. Very distressing! However, I escaped on board an American ship bringing tobacco to fair England, in order to resume service with His Grace the Duke, but we were apprehended by a British man-o'-war. And here I am, sir, your obedient servant."

He removed his large hat and bowed low to the captain.

"The court of Versailles, eh?" said Cotgrave, eyeing the snuffbox.

"Indubitably, mon capitaine."

"Nuff!" said Big Dick, and he hit the Deacon on his exposed head with his club. "The Deacon is a bird dat squawks, but I is da only one dat talks."

"Pleased to meet you!" said Cotgrave.

"Ishmael is ma next of kin. I tell you no lie, and dat's no sin. I eats no pork, and I eats no ham, cos Ishmael's daddy was Abraham. He gave him a punch and he gave him a clout, and Abraham kicked Ishmael out."

"I see," said Cotgrave.

Big Dick stopped juggling his club and rolling his eyes.

"Every day da Angel Gabriel come see me, wid twinkling stars on his shoulder, and his coat buttoned wid moons. He is der most revolutionist of all da revolutionary Gabriels of all de angels in Paradise."

"Don't talk to me of revolutions!" barked Cotgrave.

"He means revelations," explained the Deacon.

"Nuff!" said Big Dick, and he again hit Deacon John on the head. The Deacon put his hat back on.

"So what do you want?"

Big Dick began the rhymes and rhythms with his club and his eyes.

"Dis I say before I gets much bigger, dat I ain't gonna be no white man's nigger. Make da coffee and sweep da floor, chop de wood and close de door – dat's what dey tell them niggers o' mine. But no more slaves no more – dat's fine. We equal

55

prisoners, gate is lock, so you gotta put nigger in der own cell block. Den all is happy, all is nice, and we call de cell block Paradise.''

"Well, I must say that's nicely put," said Cotgrave, patting himself on the stomach and looking quizzically at John.

"We could shuffle the men around," said John.

"It will be done today," said Cotgrave to Big Dick.

"We are exceedingly grateful to you. God save the King!" said the Deacon.

Big Dick was about to hit him on the head with his club, but Deacon John pointed to his hat. "You paid for the hat," he said, so Big Dick had to be content with just bellowing "Nuff!"

No sooner had the men gone through the door and the door was shut than Cotgrave and John Adams burst out laughing.

"You couldn't get better at Drury Lane," said Cotgrave.

There was a rattle of a cart down in the yard, and a thousand voices booed and hissed. John dashed to the window to look out.

"Don't bother, Mr Adams: I can tell you what the commotion's about."

"My God! the Rough Alleys have been brought back."

"Yes, Mr Adams." Cotgrave waved a paper. "The magistrates at Exeter acquitted them immediately."

"But how could they? It was murder! There were witnesses. And God knows how many men they've murdered besides."

"The magistrates didn't doubt but that it was murder. But the judge in summing up said there was a state of warfare in which Americans were killing Englishmen, and Englishmen were killing Americans, and it was considered no crime, so how, he argued, could it be regarded as a crime for an American to kill an American? In peacetime the Americans would have been handed over to the American authorities, but there are no American authorities, so they will remain in my custody until they can eventually be handed over. I suppose there's a kind of logic to it all."

"The Rough Alleys will be cock-a-hoop! There'll be no stopping them! It'll be a reign of terror!"

"Terror outside, and terror inside – eh, Mr Adams? Oh, by the way, I put a man out to follow you when you set off for Exeter."

"Did you?"

"Unfortunately, yes. He was brought in very much like the sergeant. Looked as though he had been killed by fear – face contorted with sheer terror. Beats me how you survived, and he, who was only half a mile behind you, was slain. As I say, terror within, terror without. Thank God we've plenty o' rum and brandy!''

CHAPTER FOUR

Errand into the Wilderness

ON a Saturday morning, John again made the horse-and-coat switch at Lady Hen's and cantered on the tor trail to Sally's. He was sure he was not being followed, or rather he hoped he wasn't being followed. It was still very much on his conscience that he had brought about the death of the soldier who had been detailed to track him, and he had seen the hideously contorted face of the man. He tried to square himself with his conscience; he had not intended the man's frightful death, he had merely evaded him. But there was something else on his mind.

He had in his pocket a letter from his father:

Naturally we all sympathise with your being in prison, and you may draw upon my bankers in London for anything you need, but all of us are deeply humiliated that you handed the *Boston Trader* over to the British. Surely you could have set fire to it, or scuttled it somehow? The ship is now in service against us, and the knowledge is all over Boston. It may be difficult for you to return to Massachusetts. Your mother has nightmares that you may be tarred and feathered. This is a small but proud community, John.

The words burned into his soul. It was an accusation of cowardice, even of aiding and abetting the enemy, and from his own father and mother. If only he could take back the day he had cleared Boston and given the fatal order to his first mate: "Steer due west! Unfurl all sails!" If only – if only! Just one degree, one paltry degree, either side of the compass, and the British man-of-war would have missed him! That was a slap in the eye for the doctrine of free will. Maybe Sally was his only true constant in this world; maybe his body was just the container for a red, burning ball of love for her.

"Sit down, my love, and have some elderberry wine. You look worried to death."

She kissed him, and the world was white and clear again. There would be a full moon that night, and the sky was clear for frost. It was the night for Chagford, and the Chagford Champion would be thrown against the Tavistock Terror, she told him. The betting would be high, and there would be a large crowd.

John had no mood for a bloody cruel sport as cock-fighting, but where Sally rode, so he would ride. He was magnetised, and he knew it.

The Chagford barn was rancid with burning tallow and steaming people. The men had been otter hunting all day, and river water dripped from their trousers and formed pools around their boots. The women too were wet from working outside. The barn was festooned with candles and lanterns.

John watched Sally sidle towards two smart young French officers. There was obviously an exchange of money for the two extra horses they had brought with them, and clearly she was giving them instructions about the fishing-boat in Tor Quay, although one of the officers appeared to be flirting with her.

The two cocks were introduced to the cheering crowd. Their red eyes rolled wildly as their owners held them to be touched, petted and talked to. Iron claws were lashed to their own red claws, and they were thrown at each other in the circle. At first they walked round each other, each sizing his opponent up. The crowd made cock-a-doodle-doo noises. And then the Tavistock Terror scratched out and the fight began. John was nauseated by the fight, yet he felt it was his duty to Sally to be there, although when he looked towards her she seemed to be enjoying the flirtation. She was smiling up at the young officer with roguishness in her eyes.

Most of the women had sparkling eyes, and they were yelling cock-a-doodle-doo the loudest. The otter hunters saw the spectacle as funny and laughed at the fighting cocks. There was a group of men on their own. They were tin men; they wore iron helmets with candle-stubs in front and they were serious; John guessed they had betted heavily.

The cocks ceased to be cocks; they became one twisting,

59

turning, squeaking, squawking bundle of bloody feathers; even the feathers ceased to be feathers and became blobs of blood. One cock lay dead, the other lay dying, but the dying cock managed to sound a weak, diminishing cock-a-doodle-doo. The crowd cheered it as the winner.

The French officer, who was standing behind Sally, had his arms round her, and his hands were squeezing her breasts. She smiled up over her shoulder at him. John was enraged, and could hold back no longer. He elbowed his way through the crowd, pushed Sally aside, and punched his fist into the officer's face. The officer, although momentarily taken off-guard, retaliated with his fist in John's face. Within seconds, the two men were going for each other hammer and tongs. The crowd pushed them into the cockpit, where they carried on half wrestling, half fist-fighting as though the very devil were whipping them on. Some in the crowd yelled "Come on, Boney!" and others, being informed he was an American, no doubt by Sally, shouted "Come on, Yankee boy!", but the women screamed "Cock-a-doodle-doo." John, who never had occasion to fight much, lashed out fiercely and wildly with all the pent-up emotions induced by the letter from his father, the redcoat he felt he had led to his death, his hatred of cock-fighting and his jealousy over Sally, whereas the Frenchman had no such stimulants. John's emotions gave him the edge over his opponent. They both fought till they were exhausted, and after a time the Frenchman remained slumped. John however, was able to stagger to his knees, then to his feet, to the thunderous roar of applause from the barn. His face was a mass of blood, but it was mainly from the corpses of the dead birds they had fought amidst. It was a long time before he knew where he was. Sally, who had been busy collecting money amongst the crowd, took his arm and directed him out of the barn. There was a stream nearby. She led him to it, tore a large piece from her petticoat and bathed him with it.

"Oh, my poor dear! Oh, my darling! What on earth did you strike the Frenchman for? And then nearly kill him? Aw, sweetheart, my loved one, my heart, my treasure! Are you hurt? I could have died."

John wanted to explain but he couldn't. He began, as he had

so often done since entering Dartmoor Prison, to catechise himself. Who am I? I am John Adams. And who is John Adams? At this point he stopped; he had never gone beyond this point. And who is John Adams? And what is John Adams? And what is John Adams doing here?

"Look," said Sally, giving him a jingling bag of coins. "It's all yours. You've won it! As soon as you started fighting, I laid bets on you. It's the best Saturday night's fighting they've had for many a long day. Here, take it. You've won it."

John was still dazed as they crossed the barnyard for their horses. Sally gripped his arm and looked proudly up at him. "You're a winner, John! An out-and-out winner."

"Had a quiet weekend, Mr Adams?" asked Cotgrave.

"Yes, thank you, sir."

"Then what are those bruises doing under your eyes? Fall out of bed or something?"

"The result of a wager."

"Who won?"

"I think I did."

"For the honour of Dartmoor Prison, eh?"

"You might say."

"Hope it was with none of my rapscallions."

"The King's enemies, sir."

"Confusion to 'em, what?"

Captain Cotgrave strolled over to the window and looked out. "Here's old Dr Dyer coming up the steps two at a time. He'll get heart failure, silly old fool!" He laughed. "Tell me, Mr Adams, would you like to be physicked by a doctor whose name was dyer?"

Dr Dyer pushed into the office. "Lock the gate, and lock it good!" he shouted. "Order your guards to shoot to kill anyone who tries to go in or out! Stop the markets! Stop recruiting! Stop everything!"

"Are you mad?"

"Smallpox! There's an outbreak of smallpox!"

John sat quietly in a corner as Captain Cotgrave and Dr Dyer paced the office, sent for sergeants and issued orders.

It was decided to quarantine not only the prison but the township of Princetown, for the market people, having mixed with the prisoners every day, would surely be just as infected. At bayonet-point, nobody could enter or leave the plague area. But maybe bayonets weren't necessary; a few snowflakes were lazily drifting down, and no man in his right senses would hazard the desolate moor with the likelihood of snow, let along the terrors of hell.

"How many men?" Cotgrave asked John.

"Four thousand Frenchmen, three thousand Americans and just over a thousand soldiers."

"Nine thousand men," snarled Dr Dyer. "And once they start dying, the living will turn savage, raving wolves."

"Can nothing be done? Have we just got to wait until the walls of the prison become a tomb for all of us?" asked the captain.

"Oh yes," sneered the doctor. "A lot could be done, except that it's impossible." He eyed John Adams with a look of hatred. It was well known that Dr Dyer hated all Americans. As a young doctor, he'd been taken prisoner on the Hudson. He'd been one of the few doctors at Valley Forge, and Washington had ordered him to attend his soldiers without proper medicine, and amputate limbs with the crudest of instruments. There hadn't even been alcohol available to get the patients drunk. He blamed General Washington for turning him into a butcher who carved human beings up while they were still alive and screaming. He sneered at John: "In 1781, Mister Yankee, the British Army surrendered to your ragtag and bobtail boys at Yorktown . . ."

"Forget it!" shouted the captain.

"Can you?" the doctor shouted back, and he turned back to John. "And fifteen years later, an Englishman, Dr Edward Jenner, discovered the antidote to smallpox from the hand of an English milkmaid. Tell me, Mister Yankee, which was the greatest victory?"

"Your servant, sir," said John, and bowed a salute.

"I have enough cowpox serum to inoculate a hundred men, and that's all. I could send for serum from the big towns and depots, but there's no time, and the snow's starting. We'd need good riders and fast horses, and even then it would be touch and go.''

"I've got three despatch horses but no riders. My soldiers are infantry.'' Cotgrave burst out laughing. "God, you should see my men trying to mount. Even the horses laugh when they try. They usually end up under the horse.''

"Most amusing, captain,'' said the doctor. "I suggest you clear your head with some more snuff.''

"I might be able to get you the riders,'' said John. "With your permission.''

"Why not?'' said Cotgrave.

"Waste of time,'' sneered the doctor.

John left the office and toured the prison blocks. He came back with three men.

"Horsemen, are they?''

"Virginians,'' said John. "They'll speak for themselves.''

"Samuel Parish of Norfolk, Virginia. You see this little island of yours – well, I exercise my horse about the same distance every morning afore it gets its bale of hay.''

"Tom Rix of Alexandria, Virginia. If my horse don't go fast enough, I picks it up and runs with it on my shoulders.''

"Ben Cotton of Richmond, Virginny. I been out in the territories and the wilderness hunting the buffalo, and I tell you when them buffalo does an about-turn and comes a-chasing you, you gotta ride faster'n a fart.''

"Let's hope you can ride as well as you can talk,'' said Cotgrave. "I'll give you written authority to change horses at any depot or staging-post. And even if you don't get the serum, come back with your horses; we may have to eat 'em before winter's over. Dr Dyer will write you out an authority for the serum, I'll be bound.''

"And whatever you do, don't go inside any of the buildings,'' added the doctor. "Hand your letters over, and stay outside and wait. You may be carrying the smallpox.''

"We'll die if we die, and we'll die if we don't. That it, captain?'' asked Sam Parish.

"I want you to give me your word of honour that you'll return."

"Well now, sir," said Ben Cotton, "we ain't going to give our word to any British officer, but I reckon we'll give a handshake to Mr Adams here, Yankee though he be."

"One of you is to go to Exeter, another to Plymouth, but the most likely chance is Bristol, ninety miles away," said the doctor. "Perhaps the buffalo man for Bristol."

"Get off Dartmoor before it goes dark," advised Cotgrave.

"Damned right I will."

"And then you come to another moor – Exmoor. After that, it's hedges and ditches all the way."

The men rode out through the prison gate, but nobody raised their eyes to watch them go.

The doctor made plans for the sick, dying and dead. "Starts with a fever," he said. "Three days later there's a swelling, then it bursts, and if they're still alive, they'll be scarred for life. I want soap, alcohol, linen and male nurses."

"I don't think you'll find many nurses here," said the captain.

The doctor addressed his remarks to John. "Yankee, your countrymen are smart, or so they say, so find me some nurses. As far as I'm concerned, if they've only fanned a fainting lady with a newspaper, they're qualified nurses."

As John walked through the prison blocks, he imagined they were what charnel-houses resembled. Dead men were tipped out of their hammocks on to the stone floor, then pushed with sweeping brushes into the prison yard, waiting to be pitchforked on to a cart which dumped them in the burial-pit. Sometimes a body, not quite dead, groaned. It was the same throughout the French and British sectors, no redcoat bothered to hold his musket.

Sick men lay moaning in their hammocks, and those who were as yet untouched spent their time examining their own bodies for spots, blemishes or swellings. Many men volunteered to be nurses; helping other men die would take their minds off their own dying. Dr Dyer ordered windows to be opened and fires to be built up to keep the air fresh and warm. He told men to spread soapy water everywhere. A block was turned into a hospital, and

64

he instructed the nurse volunteers to dab patients with alcohol. There was nothing else he could do. He picked out one of the Yankees, Charles Andrews of New York, to be his assistant, telling him he'd be a smallpox doctor before he'd finished. Every man in John's block, except one or two, volunteered. The snowflakes still drifted down; the sky became heavier.

One of the boys in John's block rushed into the yard and grabbed him by the arm; the boy was wild and terrified. "Master, come quickly! Come! Inside! Inside! Oh please, Jesus!"

John went with him. The sight turned his stomach and sick came up into his mouth. Sprawled on the floor in a large pool of blood was Taylor. John had to stand in the blood to turn him over; his hands became covered in warm blood. He let the body drop back into the blood.

"I'm going mad! I'm going mad! Mom – where's my mom? Where is she? Bread and jam! Wash the pots!"

John had to drag the boy out into the yard and slap his face. "What happened?"

"It was them. They came in. I hid behind the slop-barrel."

"Them? Who's them?"

"The Rough Alleys. With Bill Jenkins leading. They didn't see me. They grabbed Mr Taylor and said they was going to show him they was back, and he could tell the others that the Rough Alleys was in charge again. Then they took his painting and flung it on the floor. Then they held him, and one by one they pissed on her face, and all laughing. Then Bill Jenkins said he could improve its artistic quality, and he took his trousers down and knelt down and shat on it. Then out they went shouting and laughing. And Mr Taylor grabbed a piece of broken mirror and hacked and hacked away at his wrists till the blood came up like a fountain and over the walls. There weren't nothing I could do."

John called for some men nearby to bring buckets of water and rags. He went back into the block and dragged the body away from the blood. When the men arrived with the buckets, he knelt down and did all the mopping and cleaning himself. He helped carry the body on a stretcher to the burial-pit and tipped it down amongst the corpses of the day. He snapped his fingers at two redcoats and ordered them to arrest Bill Jenkins. There must have been a hardness in his voice, for the redcoats said 'sir' to him and marched off to carry out his command.

The picture on the floor was shocking. He took a sweeping-brush and edged it towards the fire, but John Aikinson of Baltimore, Maryland, stopped him.

"I'm gonna clean that picture, and make Susan pretty again, that's what I'm a-gonna do."

The boy grabbed John's arm again and looked straight into his eyes. "Y'ain't done very much for us, have you, mister?"

"What d'y'mean?" John snapped.

"Up there in the office, and the captain listening to you, and him taking note of what you says, but you ain't really done nothing for us, mister. You ain't a Yankee no more. And none of us ain't Yankees no more."

"Who are you?"

"You don't even know, and I'm in your block. I'm Dan Simons of Marblehead, Massachusetts."

"I know Marblehead."

"Nobody'd think so, mister."

The boy's face was red. John put his hand to his forehead. The boy was burning up. He picked him up and carried him to the smallpox block. And then he washed himself in the stream which ran through the prison yard.

When John returned to Captain Cotgrave's office, the redcoats had already brought in Bill Jenkins and Cotgrave was walking around him as though examining a piece of sculpture. John told the captain what had happened.

"'Twas just daubing — 'twasn't no painting," snarled Jenkins. "And I didn't tell him to go and cut his wrists."

"Of course you didn't," said Captain Cotgrave, smiling in an almost fatherly way. "And I'm quite sure the painting was no Joshua Reynolds."

"What you gonna do, then? Send me to Exeter for trial?"

"Good lord no! They found you not guilty last time. And what can I charge you with? Not knowing the difference between a painting and a latrine?"

"They'd laugh at you."

"Course they would. No, sir, British justice has cleared you of

66

murder. Sir, you are innocent of all charges, and I'm going to give you your freedom. People will say I'm a fool – well, perhaps I am a soft-hearted fool. Sir, you are free to leave this prison. At ten o'clock tonight you will be escorted to the edge of Princetown and released, to find your own way home. Free as a bird, sir.''

''But it'll be black night, and it's snowing.''

''How very observant.''

''That's the same as keel-hauling!''

''Moor-hauling is probably more correct. Who knows, you may reach the coast. Take courage, sir. Captain Bligh travelled thousands of miles in an open boat. You could even take some paints and a canvas along and paint some of the interesting things you see on the moor.'' The captain snapped his fingers at the escort. ''Get him out of my sight! And see that my orders are carried out!''

Jenkins tried to kneel and grovel, but the redcoats carried him out of the office.

Cotgrave took a fist of snuff and glugged himself out some wine for himself. ''I was due to be relieved in a week's time. All this is very inconvenient, Mr Adams.''

John had work to attend to. He had to prepare a list of the dead for Mr Beasley. It was the first time he'd had occasion to look at the muster-book, and it surprised him. When asked to give the country of their birth, few had said. 'The United States of America' and many had given the name of their state. Forty years after the Declaration of Independence, the rank and file and their children were not aware they were a nation. Some had recorded themselves as plain simple 'Yankees'. There were even more who called themselves 'Doodles'. Often the country of origin was the name of the ship from which they'd been taken from; these were obviously British sailors who had gone over to the Americans and, if it could be proved, which it never was, they'd be adorning a yard-arm. The Negroes had no country they wished to claim; they recorded themselves as 'Black Man'. It made John think of the boy Dan Simons and his clear, honest accusation that he, John, had done nothing for them. He'd obtained allowances for soap, tobacco, coffee, shirts and stockings for them, he'd arranged for the Stars and Stripes to fly above the prison, but he'd not given them their nationality.

The French prisoners had no problems. They were rich and ran their own affairs without supervision. They had a history that went back a thousand years. They had a brand-new, stirring national anthem. They were proud even in prison, since their leader Napoleon Bonaparte, aside from setbacks in Spain and Russia, was master of Europe. But John's countrymen! Damned defeated Doodles.

He looked out of the window. The snow was thickening, and another thought clawed at his mind. Sally! She would be alone and isolated in the snow. How would she survive? Had he contracted smallpox and passed it on to her? Was she now shivering with fever, fear or famine? And now the brutal killer was going to be turned loose on the moor; would the moor be as protective to Jenkins as it had been to him? Would the pony-tracks and gulleys lead him to her cottage? He saw the painted face of Susan, and he saw the same picture covered with stinking brown excrement. Then he saw the face of his Sally. It was a wide-awake nightmare.

They took Jenkins to the edge of Princetown and told him that, according to quarantine regulations, he would be shot dead if caught trying to enter again. He walked away into the darkness, and the wind howled.

John flung his goose-quill pen across the room, and it made a curve which nearly landed it in Cotgrave's mug of rum.

"I know how you feel, Mr Adams. I feel the same," said the captain. "We're doomed. We won't even get food supplies if the snow falls heavy. D'y'know what I feel like doing, mmm? I feel like marching the entire garrison of nine thousand men with fifes and drums on to that damned moor and forming squares to face the devil." He shrugged. "If we were taken prisoner, it wouldn't matter, for the dungeons of hell would be better than Dartmoor Prison."

About three hours after daybreak, a sudden cheering started up; not just the cheering of hundreds, but that of thousands, roaring like a storm at sea. John rushed into the yards with the others of his block.

Riding from the gate was Ben Cotton. His steaming horse had

68

to lift its knees high because of the snow. There were sacks over the horse's saddle, and Ben had sacks tied over his shoulders.

Charles Andrews with two assistants rushed out to take the sacks. "Hell, you been faster than the wind!" shouted Andrews. "That horse o' your'n got wings?"

"'Twere just a pleasant trot through the English countryside," said Ben, "and this is me, Ben Cotton of Virginny, a-telling you. I stopped at a few inns on me way for roast beef and mulled ale, and I stopped to bed a wench each mile or so, and I came back the London way just to pay me respects to King George, him being a great friend of the late lamented General Washington. Then the King introduces me to the Prince of Wales, and we get a-throwing dice, and I loses, which ain't usual for me, so I has to become a highwayman and rob a stage-coach in order to pay me debt to the Prince. Well, 'twas a nice day, so I decided to give me legs a stretch and walk the rest of the way back home to this here wonderful place."

He rolled off his horse, and his legs gave way. He had to be helped to his block. John rushed up and shook his hand.

"Hey, I came to the right address, ain't I?" asked Ben. "This is the Prince o' Wales's Prison upon Dartmoor?" And then he passed out with fatigue.

Dr Dyer and Charles Andrews had already set out two tables in the yard.

"Right, gentlemen, form a queue for your inoculation!" shouted Andrews through a tin cone. "And if any of you wants a second helping, you gotta go back to the end of the queue. Come on, me lively lads!"

A serpent of eight or nine thousand men wound its way round the yards and the prison blocks. There were no preferences: Englishmen, Frenchmen and Yankees lined up in a laughing, shouting line.

The inoculations went on throughout the day. The snow continued to fall, and the doctor and Andrews looked like snowmen. Once a man had been inoculated, he joined in throwing snowballs with the others who had been done. The remaining two riders arrived during the course of the day. They'd both been held up by the deep snowdrifts in the valleys. It grew

69

dark with night, and still the two snowmen were screwing their syringes by lantern.

"I could have done with you at Valley Forge," the doctor told Andrews.

"Weren't born, sir. But I'm a-guessing 'twas you what took me dad's arm off his shoulder. He lived, but he weren't much good at ploughing after that. Reckon if he'd died, I wouldn't be here to help you."

An indignant Captain Cotgrave rumbled into the office. There were lumps of snow on his tricorn hat and his uniform.

"Dammit, Mr Adams, don't your Yankees ever grow up? They threw snowballs at me."

"It's a mark of affection in the United States, captain."

"Is it, by God? Then how do they show their affection in the summertime – hurl cowshit? Egad, Mr Adams, if I'd been on my quarterdeck ten years ago and some of my crew had done that to me, their backs would be smarting with the salt and lashings." The captain burst out laughing and cleared his head with some snuff. He took the cork from a flagon of Madeira, then fisted the cork back on again. "Here, you can give this to the three Virginians, with your compliments. *Yours*, do you hear, not *mine*. And I hope they snowball you every bit of the way to the block. 'Twas rum I felt the need for anyway."

The dreary quarantine period passed, but with the prison gate locked and the township cut off from the outside world both prisoners and traders ran low on food and firewood. Volunteers were turned into a shovel brigade and set about clearing as much snow as they could off the Plymouth track; it would make things easier for the relief regiment that was surely digging its way towards the prison. The cart brought in the stiffened corpse of Bill Jenkins, and as usual Cotgrave ordered his body to be put on display in the prison yard. Standing upright he was lashed to a post. The body had been found by the snow-shifting squad with its head submerged beneath the ice of Crazywell Pool. The ice had to be broken to get him out, and there was ice round his face, which gave him the appearance of one looking through glass at

70

those who felt forced to view him. His eyes were wide open, and as with so many other corpses brought in off the moor, his mouth was wide open in a silent yell of terror.

"I reckon as how he heard his name called," said Benjamin Prince of Portland, Maine.

"What's that supposed to mean?" asked John.

"'Tis well known hereabouts that if a man or maid stands a-looking down into the Crazywell Pool and they hears their name a-called in the wind, then they're off and away to die as soon as 'tis convenient, which is usually immediately."

"That's nonsense," said John. "How do they know it's true unless somebody came back from the grave to tell them?"

But in spite of his logic, John felt that if he stood by Crazywell Pool he would hear a voice say 'John Adams'.

Before nightfall, the body of Bill Jenkins was cut down and prepared for burial along with the body of the boy Dan Simons of Marblehead, Massachusetts. Now that the plague was over, the Yankees could once again return to the luxury of burying their dead in coffins. The coffins were soap-boxes stencilled *Department of Transport Soap* and there was also a stencilled crown. Usually the wording was painted out, leaving only the crown. This was done to Dan Simons's box, but for Bill Jenkins the crown was painted over and only the word 'soap' left on in order, as somebody pointed out, to let God or Satan know that the soul needed cleaning.

Neither the prison nor the township housed a clergyman, and nobody felt qualified to say a prayer at the burial. Even singing a hymn presented a problem of ethics which could have resulted in violence, for the men of the southern states were Catholics, and the New Englanders Protestants, although there were even differences between the Anglicans and the Puritans. The Puritans insisted that hymn-singing was a form of levity and an abomination unto the Lord. Furthermore, very rarely was the religion of the dead man known, and nobody felt inclined to send a man to his Maker with the wrong tune. But they couldn't just lower a box into the pit without saying or doing something, so, being in the main mariners, they settled for a sea-shanty. As the boy Dan was lowered they sang:

71

"Oh, the moon shines bright and the stars give light,
Oh, my mammy she'll be looking for me,
She may look, she may weep, she may look to the deep,
She may look to the bottom of the sea.
Oh, the ocean may roll,
And the stormy winds may blow,
While we jolly sailors go skipping to the tops,
And the landlubbers lying down below.''

A redcoat had been ordered to attend and discharge his musket into the air. John had to walk away, with tears streaming down his face; he saw the lad's eyes looking up at him and recalled his saying that he, John, had done nothing for the Yankees.

It had been a sad and dismal day, and John, as did all the other men in his block, turned into his hammock early. There was no jesting, no singing. Hour after hour he lay awake looking into the blackness, and the wind put up a perpetual 'ooo-ooo-ooo!'. Eventually he toppled out of his hammock; instinct told him to go to the burial-pit and apologise aloud to Dan Simons of Marblehead, Massachusetts.

There were a few lanterns hanging from the walls, enough to show him the way around the blocks, each lantern illuminating sloping threads of snow. The burial-pit was near the latrines, and the latrines gave off a constant stink.

"I'm sorry, Dan!" He spoke aloud, and then there was a silence in which John was nervously afraid the ghost of young Dan would answer him. "Dan, I'm sorry I didn't do enough for you. I've tried, Dan – I've tried. I've got the men more money, better footwear, coffee and soap – yes, soap. You were buried in a soap-box, a soap-box, a soap-box with a crown. Soap – yes, soap. And we fly the flag of the Union of States above the gate. What more can I give them? You said the men no longer felt like Americans. How can I give them their nationality? It's barely a nationality – it's hanging to an icicle. I'm not George Washington, I'm not Thomas Jefferson!"

"Did I hear you calling the names of two good Virginians, Yankee?"

John was startled. It was as though a ghost had answered him.

He looked round, to see Ben Cotton. Ben Cotton was undoing his trouser buttons. "Dammit but the captain's Madeira makes you want to piss like a waterfall," he said, and began urinating near the grave.

"I came to talk to the lad Dan Simons," said John.

"He can't hear you."

"No."

"Sounded to me like you was talking to Washington and Jefferson."

"I would if they could hear me."

"Jefferson's an old man, and Washington's dead as a doornail, probably trying to get a piece of heaven to declare independence. What can they tell you?"

"The boy down there said we no longer felt like Americans."

"True – I'm a Virginian. But you're a college man – you should have done more. Half the men and boys in this yer prison can't read or write. What's the good of being an American if you can't spell the word?"

"What's the good of reading and writing if we're going to starve?"

"Starve? You're beginning to think like an Englishman. Ah, mercy me! Mercy me!" he sighed.

"Where would the English be without their commissariat? Unless they can draw their meat from a quartermaster? This yer moor's full of ponies just begging to be put into a stew. Give me half a dozen Virginians, and ye'll be bursting yer bellies with overfeeding in no time."

"Thanks!" said John.

"What for?" said Ben. "I ain't given you anything."

"You'll see." John shivered, and walked back to his block. It was bitterly cold.

In the dark grey of the morning every man in the prison awoke to a strange, loud, vibrating kind of music. The music, if music it could be called, rattled against the stone walls, and men tumbled out of their hammocks. The music seemed to go through their bodies and make their teeth chatter. They pushed and scrambled to get through the doors to see what on earth was going on.

73

From the main gate marched a regiment of kilted soldiers. They were led by a bagpipe band, and behind the band marched a hundred men with shovels. The yard filled up with soldiers, and John guessed they would number one thousand and five hundred men. A command was given to mark time. They continued marching on the spot, and the bagpipes still played.

"Jesus!" said Charles Williams of New London, Connecticut, giving John a nudge with his elbow. "Them bagpipes'll sure drive to hell any devils or demons on this yer Dartmoor, for they sure put the shits up me."

John wasn't worried about the Dartmoor demons, at least not the phantom ones; he was more concerned about the new commandant. Leading the band and the regiment was a smartly dressed naval officer not much older than himself.

He watched Captain Cotgrave, now looking fairly smart, or as smart as the old man could look, step into the yard. The new commandant ordered the regiment to halt, a command that was relayed by a few army officers. The new officer smartly saluted the old officer and then, taking off his thick leather gloves, looked around at the grim prison buildings.

CHAPTER FIVE

Arrows of Cold, with Feathers of Snow

CAPTAIN Cotgrave was busy pushing and packing his personal
belongings into an oak chest. John noticed through the corner
of his eye that one of the items he included was a bag of the
counterfeit coins. Soldiers marched in and out of the office to
collect his flagons and jars of rum, brandy and madeira for
loading on a cart. Occasionally Cotgrave would snatch a flagon
from one of the soldiers, rattle it to see if it was half empty, or
sometimes pull out the cork, sniff the contents and make a
grimace before telling the soldier: "You can leave that for the
Yankees. With luck it might poison 'em."

Outside, men were assembling in rough-and-ready columns
of four, ready to evacuate the prison. For some reason, perhaps
a prisoner exchange arrangement, all the Frenchmen were to
leave for Plymouth. John noticed there were about forty men
from New Orleans mixed up with the French. Their ancestors
were French and they resented having been sold to *les anglais*
in the Louisiana Purchase nine years ago. They gave the names
of Frenchmen who had died during the smallpox epidemic.
They would no doubt enter the service of Napoleon if they
reached France. The scene below was like a Fourth of July
parade. Men hopped, skipped and leap-frogged over each
other, made taunting gestures to the new battalion and yelled
obscene words. To counterbalance the New Orleans defection,
as many Yankees joined the carnival on their way to enlist in
the British Navy. They were being booed.

Captain Cotgrave put his arm round John's shoulders and
gave him a hug. It was the kind of hug John had often received
from his father. "Come on, John," said Cotgrave, using John's

first name for the first time. "Join me in a ride to Plymouth and I'll give you my word you'll have your own frigate. The swell on the endless sea, eh? The seagulls a-squawking and the lantern dots of landfall. Parrots and palm trees, and the creaking of timbers as the ship rocks gently. It's the life for a young 'un like you – what d'y'say?"

"You tempt me, but no thanks."

Cotgrave gripped his hand, and almost whispered in John's ear: "Say nothing about the counterfeit which your eye saw me stow, and I'll not breathe a word about that fancy y'got stacked away in a valley." He winked at John, then trundled off down the stone steps to where the cart was waiting. The first thing he did was take a great pinch of snuff, then he waved for the parade to move off. On a command from the sergeant-major, the new battalion snapped to attention, and the pipe band played 'Will Ye No Come Back Again' as they marched through the gate and under the flags. It was doubtful if many understood the humour of the tune. The gate shut and the pipes stopped. From outside, the fifes and drums for the march started up, and the retiring battalion sang:

> "I'm lonesome since I crossed the hill,
> And o'er the moor and valley,
> Such heavy thoughts my heart do fill,
> Since parting with my Sally,
> Ye gods above, oh hear my prayer,
> Forever cheer and bind me,
> And bring me safely home again,
> To the girl I left behind me."

The old rogue, thought John. Could he have known, when choosing the farewell march, that Sally's name was Sally? Was it his last parting joke? The old dog, the old fox, the old wolf, the old sea dog, the old devil! I wouldn't put anything past Captain Cotgrave.

The room was empty. Even the incomplete flag had gone from the wall. Perhaps it was Cotgrave's own flag, one which had not been dipped at Yorktown. Who knew? Who cared?

The singing died away, and all sound became muffled because the snow was beginning to flake down like a blanket. John braced himself to meet the new commandant. He felt inferior in his yellow prison jacket, which he wore when on duty. The new man was smartly dressed as a fashionable young naval officer in a bicorn hat with a blue cockade, a broadcloth coat, a white lace cravat, light brown pantaloons stopping below the knee, white woollen hose, and shining black shoes with silver buckles.

"I am Captain Shortland. Who are you? And stand to attention."

"John Adams, a Yankee prisoner."

"Captain Cotgrave has spoken of you. And say 'sir'."

"Sir."

"And your duties?"

"I act as a sort of go-between."

"What's a bloody go-between? 'Liaison' is the word."

"Yes, sir."

"You're a liaison officer."

"Yes, sir."

"In that case I shall retain your services. You will assume the rank of acting unpaid lieutenant."

"I cannot accept the King's commission, sir – acting or unpaid."

"It matters to me not one jot what you will or will not accept. I am not having a liaison officer in my office who possesses no rank. Do you understand, me, Mr. Adams?"

"Yes, sir."

"The first thing you will do, Mr Adams, is have them hoist down that stupid flag from the main gate. Bless me, I thought the prison had been occupied by the enemy when I approached. Lucky for you I didn't order my troops to take up battle positions."

"No, sir. I suggest the flag remains flying."

"Your first order and you disobey!"

"There was a riot with bloodshed to get it up. There'll be bloodshed to get it down, sir."

"I don't think you appreciate the position, Mr Adams. This is

77

not a punitive regiment of odds and sods who couldn't keep their muskets clean or their boots polished. The men out there are Highlanders, the finest fighting men in the world. They took Vimeiro and marched through Spain, driving the French before them. They captured Salamanca, and now they're just back from Madrid.''

"I don't doubt you, sir. And please accept my congratulations. But the Yankees outnumber the garrison by nearly five to one. They are desperate men. They've undergone all the deprivations of hell. They don't expect to see their homes again, and they don't care whether they live or die. The will come at you like a storm wave at flood-tide.''

"A declaration of war, lieutenant?''

"A treaty of peace, captain.''

Captain Shortland looked out through the window with his hands clasped and fingers twirling behind his back, and rocked gently on his heels and toes. "The flag may remain until further notice,'' he said.

John was a little taken aback that the commandant had given in so easily. The captain turned round on him with a gentle smile. "And now, Mr Adams, we have another little matter to discuss – food and warmth. According to the London papers, this is one of the worst winters in living memory, and it is estimated there is worse to come. This snow will block the roads again, and the provision carts will not get through. On checking the stores, I find the garrison is low on food, and the wood supplies for the fires are dwindling fast. So we may starve or freeze to death very soon if the snow continues. Added to this is another small factor which must be taken into consideration. Your men, Mr Adams, are more English than are mine; this is the homeland of your forefathers. My men are Scottish men and traditional enemies of the English. Seventy years ago, the Highlanders were defeated at Culloden and massacred after the battle by the English. To a Scot, Culloden was yesterday. They have spent many years fighting bravely in the Peninsula, and they are now due to be disbanded in their homeland. But it was not thought expedient to discharge such an efficient, battle-experienced force in Scotland, so they've been transported to this place. They are disgruntled men, and are only kept in order by the discipline of their training. What happens, Mr Adams, when there is no food and no fire? There will be such a mutiny as will shake the British possessions around the world, and there will not be two flags flying above the gate, but my head and your head.''

"Just you tell that fancy foreign gentleman that I'm Ben Cotton of Richmond, Virginia; buffalo hunter, bear killer and Injun fighter of the wilderness by way of trade and profession, and if he wants them ponies killing, I'm the man, though, in my learned opinion, them ponies is so docile that if you left a musket a-lying around casual, they'd shoot themselves.''

John had already explained to Captain Shortland that Ben Cotton was unable to understand English as spoken by an Englishman.

"Plain fact is it takes me all my time understanding the talk of you Yankees,'' Ben had said. "For I'm true-blooded Virginian.''

"Please convey to Mr Cotton my deepest sympathy for his affliction,'' said the captain.

"The captain would be grateful if you would supply the prison with pony-meat,'' said John, feeling it more tactful to translate English into English by way of gentle persuasion rather than sarcasm.

"Compared with buffalo, 'twill be as easy as drinking spiced ale,'' said Ben, never looking in the captain's direction. "Them buffalo comes at you like a hurricane, and their hides is so thick you gotta wait till they're ten feet away before spinning the bullet at 'em.''

"The man's a bloody liar!'' said Shortland.

"The captain finds it hard to believe,'' interpreted John.

"Maybe I got my facts wrong.''

"Maybe, indeed!''

"What's he say?''

"The captain thinks it's possible.''

"Ay, maybe a mite wrong. For 'tis like a wind-storm them buffalo gallop, and you gotta wait till they're five feet away.''

"As long as he can hit a stationary pony, that's all we want.''

This time Ben Cotton looked straight at the captain: "If a pony

79

was the other side of a tor and peeping at me, I could so aim me musket that the bullet would go round and round the rock three or four times before hitting the pony in the arse.''

"Then let's hope he can shoot the ponies as well as he can shoot his mouth. Dismiss him!''

"Dismiss!'' said John, keeping up the charade.

"Ay, ay, Yankee!'' Ben turned and marched out.

"Impudent knave!'' growled Shortland.

"We're much more polite in New England,'' said John with a smile.

It had been John's suggestion to hunt the ponies and he'd proposed Ben Cotton as leader of the hunt. Captain Shortland had argued that Highlanders were fully experienced at shooting deer in their own mountainous country, and that they were used to snow, but John had argued back that Ben Cotton would be at home in anybody's wilderness, and he had proved his horsemanship and reliability in racing like fury for the smallpox vaccine. Shortland then arranged for five Highlanders and five Virginians on horseback to hunt with their choice of musket. About a hundred volunteers, Scottish and American, were to follow the hunters with ropes to haul back the carcasses.

"Pray God they'll get meat,'' said Shortland.

"They'll get meat,'' John assured him.

"And what then? Eat the bloody stuff raw? The fires are going out, Mr Adams. The wood stocks are finished, and there are no trees on this bloody moor. The water is frozen. Dash it all, we soon won't be able to make a cup of tea.''

"There are the doors and the gate.''

"Really, Mr Adams! I'd be the laughing-stock of Whitehall – the commandant who removed the gates and doors of his prison, and told the prisoners to pretend they were still there.''

"There are the soap-boxes.''

"Yes – the soap-boxes?''

"We've got a few hundred wooden boxes being used as coffins under the ground.''

"Bloody distasteful, if you ask me.''

"It's the survival of eight or nine thousand men. I would recommend digging up the coffins from the burial-pits. The

French first – they're no longer here to know. Then the British and the Americans."

"The Americans and the British."

"I doubt if nationality counts for much with the dead."

"Bloody ghoulish!"

"Better than dying of cold, hunger and thirst. And the only way, sir, to get a cup of tea."

"Call for volunteers."

"Yes, sir."

At first, volunteers were impossible to find. All the men found the suggestion repugnant; their stomachs turned over at the thought. A shout went up that it was a job for the niggers.

In less than half an hour there was a hammering on the office door, and Big Dick and Deacon John, dressed in their regalia of long green coat and tall top hat, entered. The captain, who had never seen them before, stared at them without batting an eyelid. "Yes?" he snapped.

Deacon John raised his hat and gave a deep bow. "His royal saintliness Big Dick requests that I should represent his serene personage in registering his abhorrent disapproval with the unmitigated effrontery of the white variety of *Homo sapiens* should be coerced into executing this repellent act of exhumation. *Habeas corpus* and *Floreat Etona*, of course. Furthermore, this diabolical exhumation is in direct contravention of established theosophical dogma, this latter appendix having been communicated to the aforementioned regal Big Dick but ten minutes ago by the Angel Gabriel in person."

"Da most gabriellest of all de angels," corrected Big Dick with a nudge of his elbow.

"Indeed!" said Shortland.

Big Dick juggled his club and rolled his eyes. Then he handed his club to Deacon John and clicked his fingers in rhythm. John had to hold a ledger up to his face so that the captain would not see him fighting back laughter. Captain Shortland looked seriously at the Negro, as though he were a tutor at Harvard listening intently to the dissertation of an undergraduate.

"Saint Peter up by de big gold gate, for de day of judgement he sit and wait, den when de coffins come up through de floor, he take off de lids wid hammer and claw, but if dem coffins ain't nuffin but few, Saint Peter got no work to do. So he don't earn a penny on judgement day, for if no work, den dere's do pay.''

"Hallelujah!" shouted Deacon John, raising his hat high above his head.

"He told you that, did he?" said Shortland, quite coolly. He twiddled his fingers behind his back and rocked on his heels and toes. "Well, I'll tell you something. There are no slaves in this prison, only prisoners and guards, and all prisoners are created equal. The black men do not have to take orders from the white men. But each block will have to find their own firewood, otherwise – " he prodded Big Dick with his finger – "otherwise you will be providing St Peter with work sooner than you think."

"On behalf of – " began Deacon John.

"Das nuff!" growled Big Dick, and he led the small man with the big hat out of the office.

There was silence for a moment, and John needed the cover of the ledger more than ever.

"What kind of place have I come to?" the captain asked himself aloud.

"I often ask myself the same question," added John.

There was a general forage for wood. Axes and knives appeared from their secret places, and doors were removed, but the soldiers put them back. Half a dozen Yankees with axes had to be stopped at bayonet-point from advancing on the thick oak door at the main gate. After a great deal of loud arguing and occasional blows, the faro table was chopped up. Captain Shortland decided to place a twenty-four-hour guard outside his office in case the tables and chairs of administration were seized by the prisoners.

As usual, no junior officers attached to the regiment were to be seen. They were men from Eton, Cambridge and the landed gentry, and John assumed that they spent the whole of their time in quarters having their knee-boots polished by lackeys, or else playing euchre amongst themselves. It had been so with Cotgrave's officers and it was no different with Shortland's. They were officers of the battle-line or the ceremonial parade; they did not wish to become involved with the maintenance of a stinking prison.

The exercise of digging up the burial-pit was going to be an odious one. The new doctor – Dr Magrath, who had replaced Dr Dyer – and his new assistant, the prisoner Charles Andrews, told the men what precautions to take. They should cover their hands and mouths and noses with linen soaked in soapy water. Andrews added to this by suggesting they requisition all the sweet-smelling herbs and perfumes belonging to the townsfolk, who were stocking these items to sell to the French. The French were no longer in the prison, so the townsfolk could spare them.

John had to argue. Many men were convinced the bodies should be in their coffins for the resurrection, but John said he was sure that bodies need not be wearing coffins or soap-boxes on Judgement Day; at sea, men were sent overboard in weighted hammocks or sailcloth. He said the bodies should be transferred to hammocks. He convinced most of them.

A deep pit was dug in which to replace the bodies, and the men stood waiting. "You first!" several of them shouted, and John realised it was his duty to set an example by opening up the first coffin. The thought made him feel physically sick, and he sensed invisible hands pulling him back from the task, but a start had to be made, the job had to be done.

The box was hoisted up and he prized the nails from the lid and opened it. The body had been wrapped in a blanket, but part of the blanket had been torn or had rotted, and he looked down on green flesh which was disintegrating into a skull. The eyes and the nose had gone, and the teeth were apart in a fiendish grin. He felt sickness bubbling in his stomach and throat but fought it back. He had to lead the men, lead the men! The body was tipped into a hammock and lowered into the new pit, and there a cheer as men began to set about the box with their axes.

"There y'are, me merry lads," said John. "Easy as falling off a log. All you've got to do is put your mind on other things."

"In this place? Like what?" said a voice.

"Like surviving to get back to the soil of America. Course, if the job isn't up to some of you fellows from Maine or Rhode Island or Connecticut or . . ."

"Anything Massachusetts can do, Maryland can do better," shouted Daniel Nash. "Fetch me some soap-boxes!"

In an hour or two, smoke began to rise from the fires, and before nightfall the forage party returned through the gate lugging pony carcasses in addition to a few sheep which they'd found buried and dead in the snow. By moonrise, bellies were full.

The hunting party set off again after breakfast.

"If only we could get down to the slopes," said Ben Cotton, "we could have venison. I seen 'em when we were a-coming up from Plymouth, antlers a-sticking outa the bushes an' that."

"I think they belong to a duke or a lord or something," said Charles Andrews.

"I ain't ever eaten a duke, not to my knowledge," said Ben. "Guess with all that port wine inside of them, they'd be tastier than suckling-pigs."

After the party had gone out through the gate, John's first order from the captain was to put some snow in the kettle and make some tea. Over the tea, John suggested that the people of Princetown should be given a share of the meat and the wood at a fair price.

"But, dammit man, they're civilians. Since when is the army supposed to look after civilians?"

"The prison needs civilians for the markets. If they leave the moor they'll never come back, and what'll the men spend their money on? It's that touch of civilisation which helps keep a semblance of sanity."

"All right! What next?"

"It's the sanity of the prisoners which worries me."

"I agree, so . . ."

"So there are empty prison blocks now that the French have left. I'd like to start a school. There are over thirty boys between the age of twelve and fourteen among the prisoners. They can neither read nor write."

"We have children much younger than that working in the coal-mines and cotton mills up in the north of England, and they don't read or write. Reading and writing doesn't turn ponies into food, or coffins into firewood."

"What a pity we don't have any coal-mines or cotton mills on Dartmoor."

84

"So you want a school?"

"It'll help keep everybody happy."

"Are you sure you don't want a college to award degrees?"

"In time. Once everybody can read and write. You'll be a great reformer."

"Like you're a great flatterer and cajoler? Ah well, there's no harm in a school."

"And a college?"

"Whoever heard of a college in a prison on a desolate moor? All right!" Shortland laughed.

"And a coffee-house. And an assembly room and a threatre. And shops. I intend to turn Doodles into Dandies."

"With my permission."

"With your permission, sir."

"Oh, I get a 'sir' for it, do I? It's the first 'sir' you've given me since the day I took command."

"The Scottish soldiers would always be welcome, sir."

Captain Shortland rocked on his heels and toes several times. "It should be amusing. Yes it should prove amusing."

The weeks went by and the men survived. Carcasses were dragged in, as were the trees they came across. One carcass was of a prisoner who had strayed from the main party and got lost.

"He must have shaken hands with the devil," grunted Shortland when he saw the horrible twisted features of the corpse. "Hide his face – don't let men see him."

"Captain Cotgrave usually exhibited the bodies," said John. "He said that fear was the great deterrent, fear of the unknown. I'm glad to see you have a different approach, sir."

"We'll keep the men in with your coffee-houses, Mr Adams."

"Parcere Subjectis," said John.

"Et debellare superbos," finished the captain.

Dr Magrath and Charles Andrews had only seven patients throughout the great freeze, and their complaints had not been caused by the cold or starvation. They were the seven remaining Rough Alleys, each of whom had been flogged by the men and the letters RA tattooed on their cheeks with needle-pricks and

Indian ink, causing their faces to swell with yellow septic sores.

Private enterprise had already started up in one of the blocks, where Abel Akins, Clement Fair and James Combs, all of Penobscot, Maine, had set up in business on their own account as makers of shoes and boots out of the hides of the ponies. Other men were busy chipping and scraping replicas of ships from the bones. John, to his detailed specifications, ordered a replica of the *Boston Trader*.

The big freeze was endless. Many times John looked up at the huge rock of Bel Tor and prayed to the rock that the thaw would come and Sally would be safe and warm.

CHAPTER SIX

A Ship in the Air

PLIP-PLOP plinkerty-plink, plop-drip-drop! All the icicles were dripping droplets, all the inside walls were damp, while outside the snow was melting grey and there were patches where wet cobbles glistened through. There was a drizzle of rain which took away the tors; only the walls of the prison could be seen, and beyond them only greyness. The men cheered, and the two flags over the gate, which had been frozen stiff, made slight drooping movements.

Captain Shortland's first orders were for post gallopers to ride to the depots of Plymouth, Tavistock and Exeter with demands for wood, wood and more wood – wood for repairs and wood for rebuilding. John included a letter in the Exeter bag which was addressed to *The Times* of Printing House Square, London, appealing to readers to donate books and all manner of learning equipment to their unfortunate Yankee cousins now, alas, incarcerated in the Prince of Wales' War Prison on Dartmoor. There was little else to be done until requisitions arrived, so John decided to take advantage of his parole and ride to Sally. Permission was granted, and he packed the bone model of the *Boston Trader* and a pair of moccasins in a linen satchel, and strode, enjoying the drizzle in his face, towards the house of Lady Hen.

The sight in Princetown brought him to a halt. Outside every house, carts were being laden up with merchandise and horses were being reversed between the shafts. The township was evacuating. They were preparing to leave the moor in convoy.

"What can 'ee expect, Yankee?" said Lady Hen. "Most of 'em had to burn their furniture before the prison started helping out.

And I had to eat me lovely little hens – them as wasn't stolen. And with all them gentlemen Frenchmen a-gone, there ain't no sane reason for us to be staying on the moor. But I kept that horse of your'n although 'twas likely to have gone in the pot until the prison gave us meat for our bellies.''

''Where's the Jew?''

''But a few doors away. But he ain't as lucky as us'n, for he ain't got no nag, and he gotta lug all his chattels off of the moor by handcart. Still, I'm thinking the good Lord meant for Jews to carry their burdens – ain't that so? I tell 'ee, Yankee, if it hadn'a been for a couple o' them new Scotchies keeping me warm o' the nights, I'd be a dead un by now.''

John rushed round to the Jew's house. The old man was tying up rolls of cloth.

''Moses?'' asked John.

''You call me Moses, they call me Moses. I am not Moses.'' He gave a little laugh and a thin white line of teeth showed from inside his great black bushy beard, a beard that went over his chest. ''But my name you would not be able to pronounce, so I am Moses. Yes, I am Moses, the Jew of Dartmoor.''

''Don't leave Dartmoor.''

''Oh no, I stay on Dartmoor and live on rocks. I eat rocks for food. Let me tell you, my friend, that rocks is bad for the digestion. The true Moses used rocks for the Ten Commandments – it is good. But this Moses of the moor finds that rocks is hard to swallow.'' He shrugged. ''I leave the moor.''

John brought his two gifts from the satchel. ''Look at these, Moses – look at these. Look at the workmanship.''

Moses put on a pair of spectacles which tilted crooked on his large nose and examined the items. ''Very good'' was his verdict.

''And there are thousands of men inside the prison who can make them. They can make their own ship, the ship they were taken from, so there will always be variety. Why, the very names of the ships are a catalogue of my country's new independence.'' There was a mixture of despair and enthusiasm inside John which bubbled out; he was going to use every ship of every Yankee in Dartmoor; he was going to give the Jew a broadside of words. ''There's *Enterprise, Tyger, President, Herald, Huzzar, Frolic,*

88

Invincible, Chasseur, Fox, Greyhound, Victory, Paul Jones, Star of New York, Chesapeake, Mammoth, Flash, Snapdragon."

"Sure, sure," said the Jew.

"There's *Hawk, Mary, Mermaid, Spitfire, Rattlesnake, Bunker Hill, Industry, True Blooded Yankee, Messenger, Formidable, Ida, Fairy, Pike, Nonesuch, Tom Thumb, Volunteer.* This is the United States of America in bone, Moses!"

"Sure. I hear."

"And there's *Fair American, Growler, Prosperity, Yorktown, Alfred, Saratoga, Lion Zebra, Scorpion, Derby, Firefly, Virginia Planter, Meteor, Terrible, Ajax, Hunter, Revenge.* Think of it Moses, all these ships taken by the British, and all the crews inside the prison. Models of these ships would be real prizes. They could decorate the homes of the English. And the men can make tobacco-jars and jewel-boxes with the British and American flags on. And look at these moccasins, Moses! See how well made they are! We can make shoes and boots and satchels and pouches and hats. Moccasins as worn by the noble savages of America; shoes as worn by the refined ladies of Boston and New York. And, seeing that they will be made inside the Prince of Wales's establishment, you could say 'Royal Patronage'. I am prepared to offer you the sole agency – retail our products where you will. What say you?"

Moses untied the roll of cloth. He raised his eyebrows. "What is tied can be untied," he said.

"Come with me!" shouted John, and he bundled the old man out into the road, grabbing his market handbell as he did so. He rang the bell loud and long until the crowds gathered around him.

"Don't leave Dartmoor!" he shouted.

"We'll die if we don't," somebody shouted.

"Ladies and gentlemen! The people of my country – relations of yours – built towns in the wilderness with commerce and industry. They were subjected to winters just as severe as this. But the summers were pleasant – apart from Indian raids. We have become so successful that we are now a nation on our own. Don't abandon Princetown!"

"We've no furniture. And the Frenchmen have all gone and taken their money with them. There's no future on this bloody moor!''

"The Yankees are here. And we'll soon have more money than the French. And the Yankees will make all the furniture you could wish for when the wood comes. And the wood is coming, believe me! Here is Moses, and he's staying. Ask him!''

The crowd turned to look at the old Jew.

"Sure. And why should I leave the moor?'' shrugged Moses.

"Hey!'' shouted the loudest voice in the crowd. "If the Jew is staying, there must still be gold on Dartmoor!''

In the English fashion, the men adjourned to the Plume of Feathers to debate upon it, although there was no doubt in the air that they had decided to stay a little longer at least.

"The sole agency?'' said Moses.

"Exclusive,'' said John. Then he saddled his horse and spurred it on across the moorland.

He had decided how he would greet Sally. He would be friendly, just a little more than friendly. He would ask her how she fared, and she would offer him a mug of wine, but he would drink only one mug. He would tell her about his schemes for the prisoners; she wouldn't be interested, of course, but he'd tell her nevertheless. In any case his mind was swimming with excitement over the schemes and he wanted to talk about them. Perhaps she would find his conversation tedious and be only too glad when he got up to return to the prison. The prison was now his home, and he felt like a young man who had left home.

Predictably, the horse sped like the wind up hill and down dale until it stopped of its own accord before Sally's cottage. John flung himself off its back, scrambled through the door and banged his knee against the table to get to her. She had her back turned and was stirring something in a large earthenware pot. He squeezed his arms round her and clutched her breasts. "I love you! I love you! Oh God, how I love you!'' he gasped in her ear.

She turned slowly round to him, her eyes looked deep into his, and she stroked the back of his hair. "Of course you do, my darling. Of course you do,'' she whispered.

"I've been so worried about you.''

"And that's how it should be, But there's never any need to worry about me, John. I've been as snug as a bug in a rug. 'Tis

90

I who's been worrying over you – the smallpox, the cold, the hunger! You poor thing! I think you want a mug of hot gorse wine, or maybe hot mead."

They lay in bed together as the moon curved across the sky and began to sink behind a western tor, throwing its silhouette to twice its size. John felt delightfully weak and relaxed with contentment. There was still enough moonlight glow to light her face and make Sally look younger than he'd ever seen her. He raised himself on an elbow and looked into her eyes.

> "I prize thy love more than whole mines of gold,
> Or all the riches that the East doth hold.
> My love is such that rivers cannot quench,
> Nor ought but love from thee, give recompense."

"Oh my darling," cooed Sally. "You're making up pretty poetry for me. Mines of gold, and riches of the East. Thank you, John. Nobody's ever said poetry to me before."

"It's not me, Sally. It was written by Anne Bradstreet."

She jumped up and struck him in the face. "Take that! You're jealous of French gentlemen smiling at me, but there you go talking of another woman in my bed. Who is this Anne Badmeat?"

"Oh hell, Sally. She was an American poet who was born before Shakespeare died."

"And Shakespeare, I suppose, was another New Englishman? How should I know when he died? Could have died but twenty years ago."

"Anne Bradstreet died a long time ago. She was very happily married, with children."

"Not like me."

"She wrote a poem when her house was burned down."

"She'd a done better chucking buckets of water on the fire. And serves her right if her house burned down for writing words to put into your mouth. She shoulda minded her own business. Don't you ever again say rhymes to me unless they're your own." She broke into tears. "I can never match up them New Englishwomen, John. Just leave me alone!"

91

He caressed her hair and her neck. "A woman is a woman anywhere in the world, and you're a woman amongst women. I'd swap old England or New England for you."

"And Mr Shake-thing or the woman whose house burned down didn't say that?"

"I'm saying it."

"Then I'm sorry Mr Shake-thing is dead, and I'm sorry the woman's house burned down, and I forgive you. You may kiss me now."

He did, several times. No, many times, a lot of times. Later, he gave her the model ship and the moccasins. "This is my ship," he said. "It's yours."

She prodded him and teased him. "I thought you were a big captain of a big ship! Pooh, what did you do with this? Trail it across the ocean on a piece of string? Now, John, if only you and I were the size of my thumbnail, we could sail away to Lyonesse and live happily ever after."

"You don't know about Shakespeare yet you know about Lyonesse!"

"I was kidding. Of course I know about Shakespeare and Lyonesse. Don't I come from Lyonesse?"

John brandished the moccasins. "And you'll go back to Lyonesse with a sore backside if you hit me in the face again. That's what these are for." He made a move to grab her but she slipped under his arm.

The cottage was filled with Sally's laughter. They didn't stop laughing until they were exhausted; life was wonderful, and love life even more so.

"John!"

"Yes."

"Would you do anything I asked, if I asked?"

"Such as what?"

"I don't know. Such as anything."

"Haven't I done everything you asked so far?"

"So far, yes. But I'm thinking of the future. Go on, promise me."

"Why should I promise you?"

"Because that's all I've got now – your love. There's nothing to keep me on the moor. The French have all left. Why don't you Yankees escape?"

"Because there's a difference between thirty miles of sea and three thousand."

"So you see, John, I know you love me, but I would have your promise to strengthen me."

"All right, sweetheart. I promise I will obey you in all fair command."

She closed her eyes. "I'm happy, John."

"Who'll buy nice hot plum-dudgeons for a penny apiece? Just a-smoking from the pan! Oh, oh, oh! My brown plum-dudgeons, crisping nice and smoking hot!" William Saunders of Kennebunk, Maine, rolled his mashed potatoes and cod flakes into plum-shaped balls and dropped then into a frying-pan on a fire in a stone grate. The market had never been so busy, so noisy, so happy.

Henry Allen of Salem, Massachusetts, strolled by with at least two dozen knitted woollen tassel caps on his head, and twirling a cap in each hand.

"Try a cap that was worn at the Battle of the Nile, its nap carried away by the enemy's shot, leaving it in the threadbare state you see. Had I the impudence of some in the trade, I might say that this cap had a charm against danger, but I scorn to say what I have not the authority to prove."

Charles Moutle of Stonington, Connecticut, carried a large placard on his front and his back, tied with string over his shoulders. Both sides advertised a boxing match with genuine boxing gloves. He rang a handbell.

"Know ye all, short and tall, great and small, that Bob Starr and Shot Morgan are to settle the difference that is between them tomorrow morning at half-past nine o'clock at the Ball Alley, the usual place for these affairs. And as Bob is a rare one, and Shot is a dare one, great sport is expected. So now come and see this chicamaree and know it is me, Old Moutle, afflicted, who is carrying this notice. Although a little rounded in the shoulders, he's a r-r-r-ready dog!"

93

Lewis Brown of North Carolina made a noise on a trumpet to attract people to the faro table. "Gentlefolk all! Meet Lady Luck at the faro table. She's a-waiting on you. Win yourself enough to buy a carriage and pair, a carriage and four, a carriage and six, a carriage and eight! Don't hesitate, for the winnings are huge! Roll up, roll up, and take yourself home more money than His Majesty King George has ever clapped eyes on!''

At the far end of the market yard was a large banqueting table on which were roast sucking-pigs, geese, ducks, fish with sauces, sirloin and rounds of beef, and tankards of porter. *Three Shillings a Seat, and All you Can Eat, to Music Sweet* said the placard. The music was far from sweet. It was played on a fife, a flute, a clarinet and three violins by John Senate, John Wilson, Josiah, Ezekiel Church, John Ring and Peter Henry, all of Philadelphia, and they could read not one note of music. Nor could their instructor, Merlin Davis of Philadelphia, who also composed the advertising slogans for the various traders. He tra-la-la'd the tunes, and he had a good voice in spite of his many years. He insisted that the only good musicians in America came from Philadelphia, and in particular the town of Bethlehem. "'Tis only the Philadelphians knows the true value of musical instruments,'' he told everybody. "In 1755 there was an Indian attack come across the Delaware and attacked the settlement of Bethlehem, where there was trombones a-playing in the assembly hall, and they turned out and blew them trombones and them Indians ran back across the Delaware. And there was a wanted announcement in the *Pennsylvania Gazette* for a Virginian actor name of Charles Love as had stolen a small white horse and a very good bassoon. And if them things ain't appreciation of music, then I don't know what is.''

Merlin Davis's orchestra, playing with donated instruments, also made it possible to start a dancing academy in one of the blocks. With his tra-la-la-ing he taught them to play George Washington's favourite march, 'Successful Campaign', and four of Washington's favourite country dances – 'The Hay-makers' Dance', 'Harriet's Birthday', 'Jefferson's Hornpipe' and 'Fitz James'. The men learned to dance with each other, and there was some embarassment. But then cartloads of women turned up at the market to dance with the Yankees, and the Yankees took their

94

women partners to see their prison blocks and the embarrassments ceased.

There was a theatre, admission twopence, and jugglers, clowns and a reciter performed on stage. The theatre was organised and cared for by a man who had let his hair grow long and took to wearing women's clothes. He wore brightly coloured blouses packed with wool to give the shape of breasts. He'd become known as Blowzy Bet. Some men talked about him, some men didn't. To all intents and purposes, Blowzy Bet was a woman, and some other men joined him in becoming women, though none of them as flamboyant as Blowzy Bet.

The traders of Princetown were delighted with the prosperity of the market, for the Yankees demanded better quality produce and more of it. People rode up in carts and carriages to buy from the Yankees and from the traders. Dartmoor War Prison became the most popular market in all Devonshire.

But the most delighted was John Adams. He strutted about as proud as a peacock. And it had all started with the model ships. "Think of it, lads," he'd told them. "Your ships have been confiscated by the British, but now's your chance to make replicas, all flying the Stars and Stripes, and the British will pay you to let them be berthed in their homes. It'll be a naval victory for you."

The scheme was supported by old Bill Johnson of Norfolk, Virginia, for Bill had sailed under John Paul Jones in the *Ranger*, and consequently old Bill considered himself one of the founding fathers of the United States Navy. He was made overseer in the shipbuilding factory at one of the blocks, checking on masts, riggings and sails, with many a story of John Paul Jones thrown in. "Finest captain there ever was or ever will be," he said. "But sailing under him would put a man in the workhouse."

"Why?"

"Cos he sank the ships 'stead o' lugging 'em in for prize-money, that's why. Us sailors made ne'er a cent. There was Whitehaven up in that there Cumberland country. Thirty-six of us rowed ashore, and there was a hundred armed redcoats all asleep and a-dreaming o' girls, and us expected the night'd see us swinging from gallows. But the people cheered us, cos English people is only Yankees, given half a chance. 'I want you to take

95

six men,' said the captain, 'and pick primroses, for 'tis St George's Day in England and the primroses'll be out.' 'Dunno what primroses are, cap'n,' says I. 'Yellow flowers,' says the captain. Us did what us was told. 'Them ain't no primroses,' says the captain, 'them's daffodils. Still I reckon they'll do.' And he puts 'em on the grave of Mildred Warner, as is lying up in the churchyard nearby, and says as how she was one o' George Washington's grannies afore she remarried, and he'd picked George's Day in honour o' General George, who, he said, would be pleased when he told him. Then we sinks all the ships in Whitehaven, for the cap'n says as how that'll please Congress and make 'em give him more ships. And the redcoats went back to sleep and we sailed away. There 'twas, us invaded England and captured Whitehaven in order to put flowers on a grave. But us wants prize-money for these here ships, don't us, me hearties?''

The Jew of Dartmoor was an astute men; he turned up daily with a list of orders. 'A dozen of *Tyger* and fifteen of *Fox* and six of *Ajax*' and so on, and the men sang sea-shanties as they worked, feeling that their ships were once again trading.

John Atkinson of Baltimore, Maryland, had his own special stall in the market, on which he exhibited the finished painting of Susan. He had cleaned the portrait and repainted it and made it come to life. It was a beautiful work of art and Atkinson took portrait commissions. People sat to be sketched, and he painted them at leisure, always taking a deposit against the finished picture. One of his first portraits was of Captain Shortland. He had painted the captain on a quarterdeck, against a background of battered and sinking French ships. The captain paid him five pounds for the picture and had it nailed up in his office. It both flattered and amused him every time he looked at it. "You must understand, Mr Adams," he told John, "I've never been to sea. I'm an administrative officer. But no doubt I'll some day take me a wife and we'll have children and grandchildren, and they'll think I was at Trafalgar."

All this new wealth made it possible for John Adams to start up his less commercial schemes. A school, known as the Dan Simons School, was opened for the boys to learn basic reading, writing and arithmetic. Captain Shortland insisted that the British drummer-boys attend the school.

The two blocks above the school block became the Benjamin Franklin College. John based everything on the writings of Benjamin Franklin. It was the first book enrolled scholars were compelled to read, for it was gentle with humour but burning with ambition. John Adams insisted that all Americans should emulate Franklin. A man who could jump in the River Thames and swim from Chelsea to Blackfriars, who could persuade tough men in a printing-house chapel to abandon the habit of drinking ale while they worked in favour of soup, who could lead a column of infantry, who could pluck electricity from God's fearful lightning, was a man to be looked up to. John even chose the essential reading material of the college from Benjamin Franklin's autobiography, and the lending library was stocked with Adam Smith's *Wealth of Nations*, Thomas Paine's *Rights of Man*, the works of Bunyan and Defoe, Virgil's *Aeneid* by John Dryden and Homer's *Iliad* by Alexander Pope. Most popular were the poems of Isaac Watts, the poet whose works had kept Franklin inspired. On the Dan Simons School walls were bannered Watts's phrases 'How doth the little busy bee/Improve each shining hour' and ''Tis the voice of the sluggard; I heard him complain,/ "You have wak'd me too soon, I must slumber again" ', and morning lectures at the college always began with Watts's 'Our God, our help in ages past'.

The organisation of the prison, with Captain Shortland's permission, was also based on the theories of Benjamin Franklin. Each block was governed by a committee of ten elected men. A constable was appointed to keep the law in each dormitory, and responsible to him, and sharing two hourly watches day and night, were three housekeepers. The previously prevalent crime of one prisoner stealing from another was almost eliminated by the vigilance and authority of the housekeepers; when it occurred, the punishment, after trial by jury, was usually fifteen lashes.

There were now over five thousand Yankees in the prison, and most of them had work to do, for which Captain Shortland made an extra allowance of sixpence a day. The first job after the wood began arriving had been to replace the doors, window-frames, forms and tables which had been thrown on to the fires during the famine; after that, furniture had been made for the traders of Princetown. All off-cuts of wood went to the shipbuilders, for bones could no longer fulfil their orders.

John was surprised at Captain Shortland's benevolent acquiescence towards his schemes, for now that the prisoners were being schooled in Benjamin Franklin and Thomas Paine, they were regaining pride in their nation. There were no longer any volunteers for the British Navy, and ambitions were to escape. When the road-building gangs marched out every morning to work on the Plymouth road, they sang 'Yankee Doodle' and spat on their hands as they grabbed their shovels, feeling confident they were building a road to freedom. Another deterrent against joining the British Navy was money. They could now earn more money in the Prince of Wales's Prison than they could on board King George's ships; they were becoming rich Americans.

John Adams was a completely happy man. His days were exciting, and his weekends with Sally were ecstatic. He loved her more and more, and life with her was always wild, always different. He no longer needed a saddle for his horse, and they rode through the wind and with the wind over the gorse and heather, jumping over granite rocks and sending foxes scampering.

They stopped at tors, where they made love, and Sally talked to the great rocks which had been there before man was on the earth: "I fetched my man along to see you. Ain't he a handsome man, though? I'm a-thinking you ain't even seen a greater pair of lovers than us two, that's what I'm a-thinking. And I'll tell you something, Sir Rock, he's a very clever man."

She would put her ear to the rock. "The mighty tor agrees with me. He says you'm the only man for me, me dear. Come along now, we ain't said hello to Crow Tor as yet. And there's Devil Tor – he's an angry one if he's kept a-waiting for to be said hello to."

Just hours before one of John's departures for home – for he now considered Sally's cottage home – John Atkinson sold his painting of Susan. The men stood beside him and cursed him for selling it, for he'd promised never to sell it, and, apart from its appearance on the market, it was always kept in display in Atkinson's block. Most times there was a prisoner, or even a group

98

of prisoners, staring at the face of Susan with the intention of taking her image under their eyelids back to their hammocks. Her picture was almost worshipped; she was the lady of the prison. And Atkinson sold her for twenty-five pounds.

"It wasn't as if you needed the money," John told Atkinson.

"That's right. But Susan needed a home. It isn't right she should be kept in prison, but I wouldn't have sold her to none but the man as bought her. He was a lord or duke or somesuch, and he begged me to sell her. He said she bore an identical resemblance to the ladies of his ancestors, and he lived in a castle, and there were paintings in it of ladies like her, and he wanted her to join these ladies. Well, sir, something inside of me told me that was where Susan belonged, like going home, returning to where she come from, like."

"Stack me, Mr Adams! Twenty-five pounds, eh? How much d'y'think my painting would sell for?" said Shortland when he heard of the sale.

"Oh, I'd say, at a conservative guess, a hundred pounds."

"Only a hundred?" he said with a wink. "Gad, sir, it shows me at Trafalgar."

"But you weren't there."

"That's what makes it unique. You've heard of the enigma of the Mona Lisa's smile. Well, there's the enigma of my smile. And what's behind my smile? Well, while all my future family will think I was with Nelson at Trafalgar, I shall know I bally well wasn't."

"Put it that way, I should say it's priceless."

"Pour out the tea," said the captain. "I've got some good news for you."

John picked up the silver teapot. "The war's over?" he asked, with such excitement that he over-poured and the tea ran over the sides of his cup.

"Near enough," said Shortland. "Some months ago, General Ross left France with a brigade of battle-experienced soldiers. They landed in Bermuda, and now they've invaded the very belly of your country. Latest despatches claim that the town of Washington has been taken and the White House put to the torch. Your President Madison and his family and his government fled so fast that they left their dinner on the table for the British officers to enjoy. It's nearly over.''

"And that's good news?" said John, putting down the teapot.

Shortland picked it up and continued pouring out the tea. "What's more," he went on, "your councils in New York and all over New England are debating on the possibility of returning to the Crown. Just think of it, Mr Adams, you may end up as George Washington began – a British officer, leading your men out to fight the real enemy, Napoleon Bonaparte. Back to the family, eh?''

John lost his temper. "My fathers fought for an independent United States; I was born in that independent United States; the men out there in the prison yards are my family!" he yelled.

"All right, all right!" snapped Shortland. "I respect your views, even though they're damned childish!" It was his turn to over-pour the cup. When he saw two pools of tea, he suddenly burst out laughing. "Like that affair at Boston, eh? A waste of good tea!''

John saw the funny side of it. "Let's say we agree to differ," he said.

"And let's say we make a fresh pot of tea and start again without spilling any," added Shortland. He rocked up and down on his heels and toes while John put the iron kettle back on the fire. "There is, however, one little matter about which we can't disagree.''

"I should be glad to hear of it.''

"The church.''

"The church?''

"You know what a church is?''

"Of course I know what a church is. I thought you said we'd be in agreement?''

"The French laid the foundations of a church just outside the main gate. Your Yankees have recently displayed such skill and handicraft, d'y'think they could devote a little of those skills, when not employed in gaining profit, to building a church for the greater glory of God?''

"I'm sure they'd be delighted as long as it can be agreed that God is neither an Englishman nor an American.''

100

"You have my word on his strict neutrality," said Shortland, raising his hand as though taking an oath.

"But best build the church fast, otherwise Dartmoor will make pagans of us all."

"And where were you when your country was in peril? Oh, I was building a church in England! Oh Sally, I'm so defeated."

"Then let's be away! As I've said, my work on Dartmoor is finished. I'll come with you to New England. Let's go!"

"I can't. I've given my word of honour."

"Who to? Your enemy?"

"To nine thousand Yankees. My work on Dartmoor is just beginning. I've helped them regain their birthright. They're returned to civilisation. They've got a school, they've got a college, people are sending us books, they've developed skills, they're earning their money, they're buying food and ale. They know they're Americans. If I left them, it could go back to the Rough Alleys and murder, and the faro tables."

"Then build your church. But before that, give me a kiss."

CHAPTER SEVEN

Diabolical Molestations

EVERY evening at twilight a solitary bagpiper played a lament upon the prison ramparts. It was the saddest music John had ever heard. But then the Highlanders were the saddest men he'd ever known; their songs were always full of exile and parting.

> Thou'll break my heart, thou bonnie bird,
> That sings beside thy mate,
> For sae I sat, and sae I sang,
> And wistna 'o my fate.

Many of the Highlanders paid their fees and attended the Benjamin Franklin College, and it seemed to be only in the lectures they came alive. John gave some of the lectures himself, although there were some schoolteachers among the prisoners.

"And this is what Mr Adam Smith, who was born at Kirkcaldy in Scotland, had to say about the English attitude toward the Amercans colonists," he began in one of his lectures, and he read from *The Wealth of Nations*:

"For next to no price England took a fictitious possession of the country. The land was good and of great extent, and the cultivators having plenty of good ground to work upon, and being for some time at liberty to sell their produce where they pleased, became in little more than thirty or forty years so numerous and thriving a people, that the shopkeepers and other traders of England wished to secure themselves the monopoly of their custom."

And John read from Thomas Paine:

"When it can be said by any country in the world, my poor are happy;

neither ignorance nor distress is to be found among them; my jails are empty of prisoners; my streets of beggars; the aged are not in want; the taxes are not oppressive; the rational world is my friend, because I am a friend of happiness. When these things can be said, then may that country boast its constitution and its government.''

There were 'ayes' and grunts of agreement from the Highlanders, and John was aware that what he was teaching would be considered by Captain Shortland to be seditious.

"Will ye tell me, Mr Adams, if there is any way that me and maybe a wee group of ma friends can become Yankees?" asked Sergeant Fraser.

"No problem," replied John. "All you've got to do is get to America.''

"Impossible. Is that it?''

"About it,'' said John. "If it were possible, we'd all be home. If you deserted, the moor would kill you, or you'd be captured and shot. How many friends would join you?''

"I'd say about one hundred and twenty.''

"It's more than I'd call a wee group, sergeant.''

"Och, man, we've got tae do something. We'll ne'er see Scotland again, for the English will'na allow it. We've fought well for 'em in Spain, and we've sent Napoleon o'er the mountains for 'em, but there's nae thanks from the Sassenachs. From here it'll be away back to France or India or Ceylon or Australia, or the Americas. They'll keep us in the battle-line till we fa' dead one by one wi' our muskets in our hands.''

"There's talk of New England returning to the Crown," said John, "so we'll be in the same boat, I guess.''

"Och, that ye will, Mr Adams. They'll ne'er let you go back to your rebel land once they've trained you in their squares and lines and guns and drums.'' The sergeant sighed. "If only we could get tae America, we could maybe send for our wives and sweethearts.''

John gripped the Highlander's arm with sympathy. "There's nothing I can do, sergeant.''

About a week later, Ben Cotton pushed John into the coffee-house. "I've been talking to Sergeant Fraser," he began.

"So have I," said John.

103

"And we've solved the problem. There's as many Virginians as would change places when the regiment marches out."

"Why, for God's sake?"

"Cos we ain't runners, see. And all we ever done in Canada was run – damn near swam Lake Erie to get away. And why did we run? We ran cos our officers ran, and they ran cos General Dearborn ordered 'em to. And if we go back, they'll call us cowards and runners. No sir, we ain't runners. The great British surrender was in Virginny, and the commander-in-chief was from Virginny, and we ain't a-going back till we've shown 'em we ain't runners."

"The British can do their share of running," said John.

"Only in America, and that's cos they don't understand an enemy as can turn himself into a tree or pretend to be a rick of corn. Line for line, I reckon they'll stand their ground, long as the French plays according to the rules."

"I guess anything is worth a try," said John. "You'll have to learn English drill." He laughed. "And you'll have to wear skirts and show your knees."

Without further ado, and in spite of many glances from those in the coffee-house, Ben Cotton pulled his trousers down. "Look at them knees; them's as good as a Scotchie's any time o' the day or night." He patted one knee. "This knee I once kneed up into a big bear's holy testaments, and when it doubled up with pain, I kicked it up the arse with this foot, and that bear limped across the wilderness on its way to China." He slapped the other knee. "And this knee is the one I used to break pine trees over to keep the fire a-burning; pine trees so thick as it took four men holding hands to circle round."

John made it quite clear to Sergeant Fraser that he and his Highlanders would have to live as prisoners once they'd changed places with the Virginians; they'd have to take their chances on being repatriated and they might even, as he'd told the sergeant earlier, find themselves conscripted into an American regiment if the United States returned to the Crown.

He asked permission from Captain Shortland for Sergeant Fraser to drill the Virginians in the English style.

"What the devil for?" Shortland asked.

104

"If, as you say, we become the King's colonials again, we need to be trained as fighting men. Wouldn't want to let you down, sir."

John always brewed the tea, and Captain Shortland, who invariably expressed surprise that a Yankee could make such good tea, claimed that he gave such generous concessions to the prisoners only on account of John's tea-making. Over tea John had another request to make: that the prisoner's theatre group should be allowed to put on John Gay's *Beggar's Opera*.

"Why not Sheridan or Goldsmith?" asked Shortland.

"Too gentle, too witty," said John. "*The Beggar's Opera* is full of whores and cutthroats, and the setting is Newgate Prison. We won't need a stage; we've got it all here, bars and everything. It's the humour of rebels and highwaymen. It was called a prison pastoral. Just think of it, sir, we'll be able to charge admission to Dartmoor Prison. A percentage will be donated for ale for the Highlanders." John rubbed his hands with enthusiasm. "A tuppenny fee to pass through the gate of the prison! Benjamin Franklin would have loved the idea!"

John was pleased with himself. The idea of *The Beggar's Opera* was to get men dressed as whores out through the gate to freedom. He felt it urgent to help as many men escape as possible rather than have them conscripted into a British regiment. The whores would be married men with families; they were on the top of John's escape list. Just what they would do if they got through the gate, he wasn't sure about.

Antony Fundy of New York suggested they would get to the coast, capture a ship, and head for France.

"I think you've got things a little mixed up," John told Fundy. "The French are no more our friends than the British. They will impound the ship and intern you in the blink of an eye. I'll do my best to get you through the gate, but you'll need a better plan than that once you're outside."

The suggestion of a plan came in the shape of a codfish. It was the largest codfish anybody had ever seen, almost as big as a man. It came in with the market to be sold in portions. Old Bill Johnson put his arms round the fish and kissed it. "Ain't you but a darling!" he told the cod. "Bless me if you ain't the most

105

beautiful lady what I ever clapped eyes on. If you was but alive, I'd marry ye tomorrow, for you ain't no English codfish. Goldarn it if me and Cap'n John Paul Jones didn't a-spy your grandmammy and grandpappy a-swimming off the shores of Labrador."

On making enquiries from the fishmonger who owned the cod, Bill Johnson's guess was found to be correct. There was a quiet creek formed by the River Teign from which fishing-boats sailed once a year to the Labrador coast and Newfoundland banks for the cod. They'd just put in with their salted fish and were being revictualled and resalted ready for their next voyage in a few weeks. They were obviously tough ocean-going vessels that could take the battering of the Atlantic gales, and they would be provisioned for a crossing to the American coast. Old Bill brought a flag from his knapsack which he said had been flown at the mast-head of the *Ranger* by the captain himself. It was a white silk flag with a coiled snake embroidered on it and the words *Don't Tread On Me*, and he intended that the flag should fly from one of those fishing-boats. He appointed himself admiral of the proposed venture.

Merlin Davis the music master, saw no problems concerning his orchestra's ability to play for the opera. True, they didn't understand a single note of written music but Gay had used popular ballad tunes of his day to which to put his lyrics, and these tunes, like 'Greensleeves', 'Lilliburlero' and 'Bonny Dundee', were still well known to his orchestra.

John was determined to get as many married men through the gate as possible. Instead of Gay's twenty-four women of the town, he enlarged the number to fifty, but he met with an objection when he asked Blowzy Bet to dress fifty men up as harlots.

Blowzy Bet tapped him gently on the shoulder with a flapping hand. "Good gracious me! Upon my soul! Oh, dearie me, Magnolia, don't you think there's enough of us already? Another fifty would lower the entire tone of Dartmoor Prison. Whatever is the world coming to?"

John had to convince Bet that the idea was to get cartloads of women through the gate with the crowds of visitors who would come to see the opera; that their main objective was to escape and return to their homeland and families.

"Well all I can say, Magnolia, is that they'd better escape good and not be brought back in their dresses or my sweet ladies will rip their guts open."

"Just how successful their escape is depends upon how well you dress them up, how convincing they are, doesn't it, Bet?"

"Very well, Magnolia, leave it to Blowzy Bet."

Apart from designating the family men who would take part in the escape plan, John left the casting decisions to the men themselves, and many of the parts in the opera were decided by boxing matches, for which the usual spectator's charge was made. The leading roles of Pretty Polly and Lucy Lockit were contended for by six of the men, which led to nearly a week of boxing bouts. Eventually, John Brown of Charleston, South Carolina, won the part of Pretty Polly, and Christopher Hubbard of Baltimore, Maryland, took the role of Lucy Lockit. They were two of the biggest, burliest men in the prison, and came out of their casting fights badly bruised, much to the consternation of Blowzy Bet, who folded his arms and tut-tutted: "My, my! How I'm expected to turn those two gorillas into pretty maidens is beyond my comprehension."

In between the boxing bouts for parts in the opera, there had been a special tournament amongst the Negroes. Their block was not organised on democratic committee lines like the others. They were ruled by King Big Dick, who of course received his divine directions from Gabriel, so there was no argument; except over a religious debate that sprang up between Deacon John and a new Negro religionist who called himself Father Simon. Deacon John maintained that prayers must be read only from the printed word of the Bible, but Father Simon insisted that prayers should come straight from a man's soul. King Big Dick had put the matter to the Angel Gabriel, and Gabriel had told him that such a delicate matter of doctrine could be settled only by fists. It was the best fight ever seen in the prison, and as much as one shilling was charged to watch it. Father Simon knocked Deacon John unconscious after an hour and a half, and thereafter prayers were shouted out straight from the soul.

It became the custom before each boxing bout or any other prison event, such as the game of rounders, for all the spectators to stand to attention and sing 'Hail, Columbia'. For one thing, it was a tune that the orchestra of violins, fifes and drums could play; for another, the British jeered at them for saluting 'Yankee Doodle', its being, sneered the redcoats and Highlanders, a jolly marching tune not a national anthem. So the Yankees and the Southerners joined together with

> "Hail, Columbia! happy land!
> Hail, ye heroes! heaven-born band!
> Who fought and bled in freedom's cause,
> And when the storm of war was gone,
> Enjoyed the peace your valour won."

The singing of it gave them a touch of pride, but it was hard to sustain that pride, for the smoke from the burning White House seemed to have drifted three thousand miles to get into their lungs.

Captain Shortland ordered John to have a banqueting table set in one of the yards, to be filled with the best food and drink the markets could supply. An important person was to visit the prison, and Shortland hinted that the men from Nantucket would be given their immediate freedom; the banquet would be exclusively for the men of Nantucket, and all other prisoners would be confined to their blocks for the occasion. There were about fifty men from Nantucket, but John more than doubled this number by advising men from Massachusetts to claim they were from Nantucket. "Even if you only passed through on your way to join a ship, and were thrown out of a tavern and into a horse-trough for being drunk, you're from Nantucket," he told them.

A slow and stately procession of sailors marched through the gate led by a boy's fife and drum band playing 'Heart of Oak'. Behind them followed a very elegant coach, and from it two decorated and braided admirals were assisted down. Captain

Shortland touched his cap in the smartest salute ever to be given. The navy escort and accompanying junior officers were dismissed, to be entertained in various parts of the prison, leaving one admiral on his own to join the Nantucket men at the banqueting table.

"Gentlemen," began the admiral, "allow me to introduce myself. I am Admiral Sir Isaac Coffin of the King's Navy, and proud of it. But even more proud of being a New Englander. Oh yes, all of you know the name of Coffin of New England; it's one of the most renowned names. My ancestors crossed in the *Mayflower*." The Nantucket men nodded, for Coffin was a well-known New England name. He tapped the ribbons and decorations on the his chest. "I stood with Admiral Nelson at Trafalgar, and my ship sailed alongside his at Copenhagen and the Nile. Believe me, gentlemen, many New Englanders fought well at Trafalgar. Why? Because, in spite of our differences, such as all good families have from time to time, this is the land of our fathers. Can you imagine a world without an England? Why am I here? Ah yes, why am I here? I'm here, gentlemen, to escort you through the gate to freedom, which is every American's birthright. Brave Nantucket has remained neutral throughout this miserable conflict and, gentlemen, believe me, it takes courage to remain neutral when all others follow with wrong drums of war. I spoke upon the subject to His Majesty King George the Third but one week ago. 'But admiral,' he said, almost in tears, 'these noble men from Nantucket are not with the other states, therefore they must be against them. They are not at war. Why therefore,' went on His Majesty, 'are they being treated as prisoners of war in Dartmoor Prison? Admiral,' he said, clutching my elbow, 'I want you to go down to Dartmoor in your own person, and give the men from Nantucket my apologies and my best wishes, and set them free.' So that is why I am here with you today. You will be issued with tickets so that you will suffer no molestation; you are free to find gainful employment and private accommodation in Plymouth until such times as you can obtain passage on board ship to your own dear Nantucket. Be ready in one hour, gentleman. And may I offer this toast – the King!" He raised his tankard and drank.

109

"The King!" shouted one and all at the table, draining their mugs, although most of them muttered crude adjectives under their breaths. There was a scramble as they gathered their personal bundles. Two hours later, the procession marched under the archway, the fife and the drum boys playing 'Yankee Doodle'.

That night there was a deep silence and a heavy depression throughout the prison. There was a mist, and it was chilly.

John suffered a heavier sadness the next day. In the rider's despatches was a letter from his father.

It has been published in the *Boston Journal* that you have accepted the enemy's commission, and that you have actively encouraged New Englanders to serve in the enemy's navy, prepared, as they no doubt will be, to engage with and slaughter their own countrymen. I have no alternative but to disown you completely. This is no longer your home, and may you never return to Massachusetts.

Attached to the short letter was a newspaper cutting, brown with age of a year. It told how the American frigate *Chesapeake* had sailed out of Boston harbour to engage the smaller British ship *Shannon*, at the invitation of her captain. The captain of the *Chesapeake* had been so confident of victory that his ship carried over two hundred pairs of handcuffs for the British sailors. Everybody in Boston who owned a small boat had followed the *Chesapeake* with food, ale, wine and champagne to make a festival of the occasion. But the *Shannon* had raked the American with a shattering broadside, then she had closed, grappled and boarded. The Stars and Stripes was lowered, the British flag hoisted to the mainmast, and the *Chesapeake* was later towed off in prize. The people in the boats, stunned at first, had cheered the British ship as though the whole engagement had been a friendly contest, even though there were casualties of two hundred and twenty men, and the captain of the American ship was mortally wounded.

The whole business of warfare and blood and indeterminate nationality sickened him, and his father's unfair condemnation and severance made his lungs heavy and his stomach empty. He needed Sally, and it was time to ride to her.

He walked out through the gate and looked across at the church which was being built fast. The men from Salem and Philadelphia made up most of the workers even though their views on architecture differed; some gangs dug up the stone from the moor, others shaped the rocks, others cemented them into walls. The rough woodwork was done by men from the northern states, while the finer carvings were made by the Virginians. Mariners had become expert church builders; they earned sixpence a day for their work, which they spent in the Plume of Feathers. John felt he had lost the right to look upon it as a church; to him it was building. As he looked at it, he felt he was a traitor not only to his country but to the religion of its people. Sally was more important to him than anything.

Lady Hen had changed her title to Mother Goose, for she now kept geese instead of hens.

They'm the ones for you Yankees,'' she told John. "Ain't a-bothering no more with them clickety-clickety 'my black hen what lays fine eggs for gentlemen', for 'tis 'Goosey goosey gander, whither shall I wander? Upstairs and downstairs and in me lady's chamber'.''

The geese hissed threateningly at John as he rode Prince through their gossiping groups.

The cottage was empty when he arrived. Everything was neat and tidy, and the peat fire was giving off a warm, comfortable odour. Sally was not there, and he was annoyed, because she knew he would be coming.

He sat down on the chair by the fire and lit the churchwarden's pipe which he had taken to smoking. He half dozed in the blue smoke of the pipe and imagined he saw geese spitting at him, indeed heard them doing so. Then their hoarse cackling became a babble of voices as though many were laughing and arguing in the distance. And then he heard the sound of deep breathing. At first he thought it was himself, so he held his breath, but the sound continued. It stopped, and he listened to his heart thumping; this time he knew it was his own heart. Suddenly, with a shiver, he became afraid of the moor. It was no longer a beautiful female moorland with purple hills and black tors; it was grey daylight breathing evil.

"Allee! Allee! Allee!" A hollow voice called from outside the

111

cottage. John was petrified. He knew he had to face whatever was out there. He grabbed the rapier from beneath Sally's bed and rushed to the door.

Outside was the most horrible-looking creature he'd ever seen or dreamed about. It resembled a man, but the face was black and twisted; one ear was missing, one eye was white and staring as though blind, the corner of its thick grinning mouth was twisted and two brown teeth protruded. It was a hobgoblin, a grotesque dwarf, a devil's child.

"Get away! Be off with you! Go on! Away – d'y'hear!" John yelled, pointing the rapier at the creature. It shuffled round him, trying to reach the cottage door. He lunged at it, but it continued dodging him. It grunted at him and he lunged nearer, until he was able to prod it with point of the rapier. Blood came from the arm; the ugly thing dabbed at the blood, then whimpered and dragged itself off over the hill.

John returned to the chair by the fire, but he no longer wished to sit down. He had no interest in his pipe; he preferred to pace the room, pacing it with heavy footsteps so that he could hear his own boots. He was both afraid and angry. Sally should have been there at home waiting for him. How dare she not always be there! His father had taken away his parental home in Boston; the only home he had now was the home of this girl, woman, wife, lover, angel, goddess, devil's daughter; this wonderful bewitching lady. But she wasn't here, and the cottage was empty and frightening without her; it was no longer his home.

He couldn't be bothered to light the candles and the room grew gloomy. He listened for Sally's horse, but the only sound was the wind gathering strength and moaning.

Suddenly Sally appeared in the doorway. He strode up to her and slapped her face with one hand, and as her head bent with the blow, slapped it with the other. She staggered under the clouts and looked up at him like a hurt kitten.

"How dare you!" he shouted for all the hills to hear. And then he dropped on his knees at her feet and kissed her legs, and blubbered he was sorry, was sorry, was sorry.

She stroked his hair and sat him down on his chair and poked the fire until it sparked and grew red.

"I was riding home and my horse fell in a ravine. Poor thing, she broke two legs and I had to kill her."

"Kill her!"

"What else? She would have taken days dying in pain. She showed me where there was a rock, and I used it." She burst out sobbing for the dead horse. "And I brought it into the world three years ago. Oh John, killing was the only thing." She raised her skirt and her thighs were covered in cuts and bruises. "And I hurt myself when I fell, John. I needed you, and I called out for you."

John began to smooth her hair and comfort here, although deep down inside himself was the irritating thought that she'd just killed a horse with a rock, with her own hands on a rock. "And I needed you," he told her. "There was a demon called." He told her about the imp he had wounded and chased away.

She sat up and smiled. "Weren't no imp or demon," she said. "'Twas the mundic man calling for food. He comes when he's hungry. You shoulda fed him. That was all he came for, and he'da bowed and scraped his thanks."

"What in tarnation's a mundic man?"

"Well now, there's men on this moor as gathers the bits of rock left over by the tin and copper men. They boil the rocks in a big cauldron in a cave. It's got to be white fire with lots of peat so the rocks steam and make clouds. And the mundic men gotta wear wet wool over their faces and hands, for the steam is the very devil's own breath. Then they let the fire go out and the cave go cold, and they scrape off the stuff that's left on the cave walls. It's called arsenic, and they sell it to doctors and dyers and the like. When that poor man was a baby, he crawled into his daddy's cave and smeared the stuff from the walls all over himself. 'Tis a shame; he's such a poor helpless, harmless man, he wouldn't hurt a fly."

John had a guilty feeling, but he tried to suppress it because he didn't want Sally to know about it. But Sally knew. She burst out laughing at him.

"Well, my goodness, John; there's you worrying about me killing a horse because it was in mortal agony, yet you would have killed a man because he frightened you. Oh, my-my-my!"

113

John looked away, but Sally pushed him on the bed, flung herself on top of him, climbed all over him and cuddled him. "But I'm so proud you hit me, my darling man, for it shows you love me and miss me and need me," she sighed. "And I need you. You've given me needs that ain't good for me – needs I shouldn't have. You've given me the Monday fever, for the night after you've gone back I need and I need and I need you until it burns inside of me and destroys me just like the mundic."

As always, they loved and laughed and ate and drank and wrestled and soothed and stroked, and galloped from tor to tor. There was never a fixed routine to the tors she chose; she picked them at random as the breeze took her. "And now it's off to Beardon we go," she'd say, and away she'd go faster then the wind, with John and his nag panting to keep up with them.

"Why, Sally? Why do you make such quick decisions? Why must we race from tor to tor?" he asked.

"It's my religion," was her answer. "Don't you people rush to church when the bells ring? I rush when I hear a tor call our names."

John thought of all the tors he knew, and he realised it was a religion. Just as the names of the prisoners' ships summed up the United States, so the names of the tors made up a catalogue to describe the paganism of Dartmoor. There was Wind, Hollow and Laughter; there was Sharp, Leather, Black, Chat and Wild; there was Hen, Leg, Hawk, Rook, Hare, Fur, Cut; there was Devil, White, King, Top, Rough, Raven, Hunter, Whooping, Birch and Brat. They were far from the saints' names of churches, but they were the names of the fears and deaths of the moor.

Upset by the letter from his father, and by his own barbaric treatment of the mundic dwarf, John felt mentally impotent. All he could do was answer words with words, hurl nouns at nouns, fight the names of English tors with the names of American ships.

For King he answered with *President*, for Hunter he gave *Virginia Planter*, for Brat he said *Tom Thumb*, for Devil he said *Victory*, for Raven, *Fairy*. It became a mental game to keep his brain active. When Sally shouted Rook, he salvoed with *Kingfisher*; at her laughter, he gave a broadside with *Fair American*. They shouted the game aloud, and he felt better. But

114

when one of them shouted Love, the other shouted Love, and that was the end of the word game.

He left her before sun-up on Monday. He walked the horse gently through the ground mist. The horse's knees were down in the mist, and gave the impression they were floating above the clouds. The moon was setting on the Atlantic side of the hills and the morning star ruled the sky. John went back to depression. He remembered some lines from Milton:

> The flocking shadows pale,
> Troop to the infernal jail,
> Each fettered ghost slips to his several grave,
> And the yellow-skirted fays,
> Fly after the night steeds,
> Leaving their moon-loved maze.

Wasn't that what he was doing? Leaving the moon-loved glade, and his yellow-skirted fay and himself a shadow pale returning to 'the infernal jail'? Dartmoor granite, the very granite which formed the rugged altars of Sally's primitive religion, was being broken and chipped by the Americans into Euclidean and Pythagorean shapes for a Christian church, sworn to destroy her gods. But he had acknowledged her tors, and something told him from the remnants of his Calvinistic soul that he would have to pay the piper.

CHAPTER EIGHT

Pastime and Frolicks

Come and See *The Beggar's Opera* as it is performed at the Prince of Wales's Theatre in a Real Prison upon Dartmoor, with an Outstanding Dramatis Personae of Real Prisoners. Written by Mr John Gay.

The advertisements, exhibited in Exeter, brought a stream of carriages to Princetown on the day the opera was to be presented, and both prisoners and traders were prepared for them with market stalls, which began long before the outskirts of Princetown. The first stall was set up by Jack Salter of Nashville. He sold violins that he had made himself, but since he was unable to play the instrument, he was assisted by Josiah Abraham.

"I'm Jack Salter of Nashville, Tennessee; leastwhise I think it's Tennessee, though it could be in South Carolina, for the government ain't a-yet made up its mind upon the subject. And I was invited to take up residence and make violins for you people by His Royal Very Highness the Prince of Very Wales himself, who provided me with an escort of British man-o'-wars in order that His Excellency the Emperor Napoleon couldn't steal me away, the Emperor himself wishful for me to make violins for his Frenchmen and such. And when I get back home I'm a-gonna marry a Cherokee girl, for only a Cherokee girl knows the right amount o' salt to put in a bear stew, and we're a-going to cross the Ohio, if it's still called the Ohio, and sell violins to the redskins, for it's said as how music has charms to soothe a savage breast. Now, me being busy taking gold sovereigns from off of you lucky people, my hands is occupied, so my good friend Josiah Abraham has come all the way from Philadelphia, which is in Pennsylvania, or was in Pennsylvania when last he left, in order to demonstrate what kinda tunes these violins is capable of if put to the test."

Abraham played 'The Hay-makers' Dance'.

"What's more," went on Salter, "my violins is guaranteed to play these selfsame kinda tunes without you not needing to take no tuition whatsoever. Take one away, and hear it play!"

Mingling with the violin tune was the roar of a bellows and the clanging of hammer upon anvil, for near to the stall Henry Brown, John Cox and Bill Warner, all of New York, had set up a blacksmith's forge.

"Let us cast our peepers over the shoes of your gee-gees afore you sets back over these here moors, for we'd hate to think of you breaking down in the middle of the night and being eaten up by a goblin. Me and my friends here have been born to the blacksmith's trade. Our daddies and grandaddies shod nags for Paul Revere and Dick Turpin, and the only occasion Dick Turpin was captured and hanged was the time he took Bonny Black Bess to a rival blacksmith."

Stall touched stall all the way up the road, round the corner and along the lane to the prison gate. A local trader held up a large salmon.

"This yer fish was a-swimming and a-singing its head off in the River Teign but this very morning, till it decided there weren't no better ambition for a salmon than to be served up on a silver dish to ladies and gentlemen."

Mother Goose not only sold prepared geese, but feather pillows and quill pens.

"Rest your weary heads upon these here goose-feather pillows, me lovelies, and ye'll have dreams sweeter than any what opium can bring. There'll be dreams of gold and silver and handsome men and dainty maids. 'Twill make 'ee want to write poems with one o' these here pens. And writing them poems will give 'ee an appetite for one o' these here cooked gooses."

Morris and Reuben Russell, brothers from Savannah, Georgia, operated a Punch and Judy box theatre. The constable was dressed as a redcoat.

"You've killed your wife! You've killed your wife!" piped the redcoat.

"I only killed her once, so you don't have to say it twice," squawked Punch.

117

"Then I'm taking you to Captain Shortland."

"Oh no! Not the wicked Captain Shortland! Feed me to the alligators, throw me to the lions, but don't take me to Captain Shortland!"

Inside the prison the bagpipes played 'Bonny Dundee', and in a corner of the first yard a group of Highlanders took turns to dance over crossed swords.

Blowzy Bet and his team had turned men into women with perfection; perfection but without enthusiasm. They took more interest in making the men look like cutthroats and pickpockets.

"Oh my goodness, what a dashing young fellow you are," said Bet as he gave Christopher Hubbard of Baltimore, Maryland, a final scar of charcoal, turning him into Crooked Finger Jack; and then Bet kissed him on the lips. Christopher Hubbard sprang up from the chair and shook his fist under Bet's nose.

"Do that once more, and I'll put me arm down your mouth, pull out yer guts, and turn you inside-out till you looks like a skinned rabbit."

"Oh, what bullies some of you men are," said Bet, flapping his hands.

Ben Cotton had been persuaded to play the highwayman's part, the lovable scoundrel Macheath, and Bet had succeeded in enhancing his features; he looked twice as brave and twice as handsome.

In that part of the yard where the acting was to take place, a gallows had been erected, with an execution cart beneath it. In front of that was a banqueting table filled with flagons and mugs.

The audience, numbering about a thousand, had to stand around the acting area. In the front ranks were important men like officers, officials, magistrates and clerks with their wives or ladies. It was unlikely any of them had ever seen *The Beggar's Opera* and therefore they were innocent as to the kind of bawdiness they were in for.

One of the first references in the opera was to a man whose occupation it was to get women prisoners pregnant in order to avoid their being hanged by the neck. This caused a nervous fluttering of fans from the ladies in the front rows, and coarse laughter from the women near the back of the crowd.

118

"If none of the gang takes her off, she may, in the common course of business, live a twelve-month longer. I love to let women escape. A good sportsman always lets the hen partridge fly, because the breed of the game depends upon them," said Peachum the bounty hunter and receiver of stolen property. "There is nothing to be got by the death of women – except our wives."

A lady, who had been holding a large salmon wrapped up in linen like a baby, gave it to her husband and walked away from the audience.

John Adams, who had positioned himself at the side of the acting area, began to wonder if he had chosen the right play. The actors were acting too well, and seemed to relish everything they said.

"Tell me about the gang," said Mrs Peachum. "I do hope you're not going to turn Bob Bounty in for a reward."

"I have set his name down in the blacklist – that's all, my dear. He spends his life among women, and as soon as his money is gone, one or other of the ladies will hang him for the reward, and there's forty pounds lost to us for ever."

"You know, my dear," smiled Mrs Peachum, "that I never meddle in matters of death. We women are bad judges, for we are so partial to the brave that we think every man handsome who is going to be a soldier in the army or a corpse on the gallows."

More ladies in the front shuffled away to the back and began examining the building of the prison. Some of them returned, however, when Macheath made his entrance and started to tell Pretty Polly how much he loved her, and how he'd just married her. And the opera suddenly became alive when they sang their first duet:

"I would love you all the day,
Every night would kiss and play,
If with me you'd fondly stray,
Over the hills and far away."

An addition had been made to this scene. All the whores danced on and repeated the song with emphasis on 'Over the hills

119

and far away', pointing to the prison gate as they did so. John was nervous that they might be giving the game away about their proposed escape.

The play continued. Mr and Mrs Peachum were concerned about their daughter Polly marrying the highwayman, but assumed that, like any sensible woman, she would get her hands on his hold-up loot, then turn him in for the forty pounds hanging money and become a rich widow as soon as possible. The ladies in the audience tittered, but they were waiting for Macheath to reappear, which he soon did in a scene of his own. He had a fair singing voice and he addressed his song personally to each fine lady in the front row, causing her to blush and step slightly behind her husband or escort.

> "If the heart of a man is deprest with cares,
>   The mist is dispell'd when a woman appears,
>   Like the notes of a fiddle, she sweetly, sweetly
>   Raises the spirits and charms our ears,
>   Roses and lilies her cheeks disclose,
>   But her ripe lips are more sweet than those.
>   Press her, caress her with blisses,
>   Her kisses dissolve us in pleasure
>   And soft repose."

There was one song, however, which was sung to perfection, and it made John long for Sally.

> "Youth's the season made for joys,
>   Love is then our duty;
>   She alone who that employs
>   Well deserves her beauty.
>   Let's be gay
>   While we may;
>   Beauty's a flower despised in decay.
>   Youth's the season made for joys,
>   Love is then our duty."

A tender hand gripped his arm; it was Sally. She had come to see the opera and she looked lovely, nicer and smarter and prettier and more colourful and more wonderful than any single one of the officers' partners; there was more beauty in her than in a dozen fine ladies. She looked up at him and sang:

"Hark the tiny cowslip bell
In the breeze is ringing.
Birds in every woodland dell,
Songs of joy are singing.

"That's the tune I've always known, John! Known since I was a little girl. I must learn the opera words and sing them to you when you are contented and sitting before the fire, drinking a mug of my wine and smoking your new clay pipe. Won't that be heaven?"

She squeezed his hand, and he felt that they were in bed together before this prison audience. He blushed and felt himself go hot, yet he dared not let her hand go.

"Let us drink and sport today,
Ours is not tomorrow.
Love with youth flies away;
Age is nought but sorrow.
Dance and sing;
Time's on the wing;
Life never knows the return of spring.
Let us drink and sport today,
Ours is not tomorrow."

"D'y'hear that, John? Oh, d'y'hear that? Ours is not tomorrow!" There were tears glistening in her eyes.

John instinctively put his arm round her and kissed her on the lips. What did he care if the whole of Dartmoor Prison was watching him, or the whole of England, London, Boston, the entire population of Massachusetts? Let them look: he loved her.

But nobody noticed them. All eyes were on Ben Cotton as Macheath.

"I must have women!" shouted Macheath, slapping his thighs

121

and looking straight at a pretty young lady who was holding on to the arm of an officer from the Hussars. The officer gave a thin smile to let people see it was all in jest.

The whores came on, and at the end of the scene they did a whores' dance to a sedate minuet, waggling their bottoms and hoisting up their false breasts.

There was a loud pistol-crack which echoed between the prison block walls, and Macheath swaggered forward brandishing a pistol. He sat on the table and reloaded the weapon.

This stupid act of bravado, John thought, would thwart the entire escape plan. The officers in the front ranks put their hands on their sword-hilts, and several Highlanders on the walls gripped their muskets tighter. This would put Ben Cotton in the *cachot* for three months for stealing a weapon and the entire performance could be stopped any minute. He pointed the pistol at the head of Lord Clifford, a local lord, and caused audience, cast and guards to tighten up as though frozen solid; there was complete silence. Then Macheath shrugged to his gang of cut-throats and handed the pistol politely over to a Dragoon officer.

"I beg you, gentlemen, act with conduct and discretion. I don't need a pistol," laughed Macheath.

There was a wave of relieved laughter, and as this was followed by the Dance of Prisoners in Chains, the whole production reached a new height of entertainment.

Macheath was arrested and condemned to death, but he made love to Lucy Lockit, the prison-keeper's lovely daughter, and persuaded her to unlock his chains.

Lucy Lockit and Pretty Polly become passionately jealous of each other, and Lucy poisons the gin; but Polly won't drink the gin, and the jar is left on the table. The whores added an extra scene of their own by sneaking in and supping a mouthful of gin, then holding their throats and doing a death dance.

But of course Macheath is finally betrayed by another whore. There is talk of a reprieve so that Macheath can be transported with his wife. But which wife? Polly or Lucy Lockit? Eight other wives, carrying bundles supposed to be babies, rush in and claim to be his lawfully wedded wife, each and every one of them.

"This is too much!" shouted Macheath. "Here – tell the

sheriff's officers I am ready!'' He jumped up on the execution cart and put the noose round his neck. Then a beggar stepped from behind the cart.

"This is a downright deep tragedy, for an opera must end happily. So – you rabble there – run and cry a reprieve. Let the prisoner be brought back to his wives in triumph. Come on there, you scurvy rabble,'' shouted the beggar, pointing to the audience. "Shall he hang?''

"No!'' shouted the women in the audience, including the gentle young maidens who had previously blushed and hidden behind their men.

"Shall he go free?''

"Yes!'' shouted the women, most of them receiving looks of censure from their escorts.

"Yes!'' shouted Sally, and John squeezed her hand tight till it hurt.

The Beggar's Opera ended to loud applause, and the bagpipes played "Will Ye No Come Back Again'.

In the rattle, rush, noise and confusion to be off the moor before nightfall, John saw the painted whores packing themselves into some of the carts, including the execution cart. They went out through the gate in the general tumult, and John noticed that one or two of the whores blew kisses to the Highlanders, and the Highlanders blew kisses back, which was high credit to Blowzy Bet's make-up ability, for some of the whores were the toughest bunch of seamen who had ever sailed the seven seas.

John showed his parole pass at the main gate and he rode home with Sally.

They didn't speak on the journey, but no sooner had Sally entered her cottage than she flung herself down on the bed. "Oh, John, didn't you hear it? 'Let us drink and sport today, ours is not tomorrow!' Oh John, I'm sorry for what I done to you, truly I am.''

"Why? What have you done?''

"I caged a hawk. I turned you over to the redcoats because I wanted to keep you on the moor.''

"We've gone over that, and it seems to me it was a good thing. Men and women singing their heads off and enjoying themselves.

A school, a college, coffee-shops, prisoners earning their own living as independent men. Thanks to you for turning me over to the soldiers. It was meant to be.''

"You don't mean that.''

"I do. Thanks for being you.''

"And thanks for being you. 'Youth's the season made for joys, love is then our duty'.''

"Let's not neglect our duty.''

Captain Shortland had not attended *The Beggar's Opera*. The next morning, he was in the office before John and had made the tea. He indicated there was enough in the pot for John.

"You missed good entertainment yesterday," John began. "My guess is it's the first time opera's been performed on Dartmoor.''

"I have seen dancing bears who shit on the audience during their act, performing dogs who started to copulate half-way through the act, bad-tempered mummers when Joseph started a fight with an angel, and fire-eaters who accidentally set fire to themselves, Mr Adams, and I'm sure your popinjays came nowhere near their high standard.''

"We took twelve pounds ten shillings at the gate.''

"As this is a prison and not Drury Lane, you may allocate the money towards prisoners' Christmas comforts, although they seem to be better off than most ordinary Americans or even ordinary Englishmen.''

"Thank you. And on the debit side . . .''

"Debit side? Don't you tell me your Yankees have made a loss?''

"No, sir! You have. You've lost forty-seven prisoners.''

Shortland spluttered tea. He was silent for a minute; his eyes looked up to the oil painting of himself.

"So *The Beggar's Opera* was a ruse to help prisoners escape, and it was all cunningly worked out, wasn't it? Nothing to do with twelve pound ten shillings!''

John said nothing at first, and then: "The men felt it was their duty to escape.''

124

"Did they?"

"Yes, sir."

"If I recollect, more women seemed to leave the prison than entered it. I watched the carriages and carts as they left. One brazen-faced hussy waved to me. That's it. They left disguised as whores. Well, I sincerely hope that the press-gangs get them in the female clothes they're wearing, with their painted cheeks and lips, and their earrings. There'll be a few surprises when they're dumped in a British warship dressed as whores."

John gulped at the thought. "Yes, I suppose there will."

"And my name will be a cause for merriment in the saloons of Plymouth, Portsmouth and Greenwich." He prodded John with his finger, rocked on his heels and toes, and his mood blackened. "Only sixty years ago, Admiral John Byng was executed on his own quarterdeck. Shot in the head, by gad, not for treason, not for cowardice, but for failure, simple failure, nothing more nor less. Let me assure you that your escape must be a complete success, for if one prisoner is recaptured, just one, and a charge is made against me, then my last duty will be to haul you in front of a firing-squad down there. Drink your tea before it gets cold."

The day of Christmas Eve was heavy in the prison. The Americans had everything except freedom, and they couldn't understand it, for there was no war in Europe, since Napoleon had abdicated and gone into exile at Elba; yet their country was still at war with England. Each man felt he had been doomed to life imprisonment; there were no trumpets to blow down the walls. They had worked hard to finish the Princetown church. It might have helped if they could have celebrated Christmas in the church, no matter how long and dreary the minister's sermons; but the church was still a few weeks from completion. They shuffled and trudged around the yards in pairs. They walked in a veil of drizzle and talked about the snows of New England.

Before dark in the afternoon, the prison bell clanged for assembly and the men, hands in pockets and heads on their shoulders, mooched into groups.

Captain Shortland stood outside his office and shouted down to them through the cone: "I am empowered to inform you that this evening in the seaport town Ghent, in Belgium, a treaty of peace

125

will be signed between his Majesty's government and the States of America. A fast ship, *Favourite*, is standing by to take this treaty under full sail to America to be ratified by your Congress. You are to do nothing until further instructed. You must remain as you are until otherwise ordered. The world is now at peace. Gentlemen, I wish you merry this Christmas!''

There was a few seconds' silence, and then the roar of six thousand men came like a sudden storm at sea. Men jumped and danced, kicked each other, punched each other, kissed each other. They whooped, yelled, screamed, whistled and laughed. Bagpipes played different tunes. It began with ten men, then fifty men, a hundred men, five thousand men all singing:

> "Deck the halls with boughs of holly,
> For-a-lolla, lolla, lolla, lah!
> 'Tis the season to be jolly,
> For-a-lolla, lolla, lolla, lah!''

And from there to:

> "The rising of the sun
> And the running of the deer,
> The playing of the merry organ,
> · Sweet singing in the choir.''

The Scotsmen were silent; these carols were unknown to them; they were old English carols, which the Americans knew.

Food and drink were brought out from secret stores; the men ate venison, pork, beef, mutton and salmon; they ate and ate; there was no further need to hoard food. Every lantern was lit to the full; it was unnecessary to save oil. The orchestra played every tune they could think of. Bones and pieces of wood used for the model ships were thrown on the fires to make the blaze crackle. Items, once precious to their owners, were auctioned off at impossibly high prices, for English money ceased to be of value in their eyes. On and on went the celebrations throughout the night. Song after song was sung; the Highlanders danced sword dances with their hands high above their heads; men who had

126

derided Blowzy Bet's ladies now danced barn dances with them. Men were physically sick from too much food and drink.

Somebody put a roasted partridge in John's hands; somebody else gave him a mug of French brandy. Yet of all the men in Dartmoor Prison he was the only sad one; the food and drink could go to waste as far as he was concerned. It was finished. His services would no longer be required at the prison, for it was no longer a prison. His father had disowned him; Boston was no longer his town; he had no ship. He loved Sally so much that she felt a part of him, yet they couldn't just live out their lives on the moor, make love, swim in streams, gallop up tors. He needed employment for his brain. If she loved him as he loved her, then she must, must, must sail with him in somebody else's ship to the New World and a new life.

A streak of greyness came into the sky, and a few men shivered; and then the ship carol started a commotion:

> "I saw three ships come sailing by
> On Christmas Day, on Christmas Day,
> I saw three ships come sailing by
> On Christmas Day in the morning."

The words 'ships' began it. Men rushed into their blocks and made kitbags out of hammocks. They packed and prepared to leave, for the ships were coming to take them home. The ships would be there for them on Christmas Day in the morning. They babbled to each other about the first things they would do when they arrived back in Charleston, Norwich, Baltimore, Pelham, New York, Philadelphia, Portsmouth, Salem and Boston. They gossiped about subjects which for three years they'd kept to themselves. Was Bill Dawson still the finest axe thrower in Maine, or Tom Spalding the champion horseshoe pitcher in Rhode Island? Had their houses and barns stood up to three winters? How were the tobacco and cotton crops? Were there still the notorious tavern fights in Nantucket on Saturday nights?

They pushed and jostled each other to get out through the doors and into the yard. Some spat on the prison floors; others urinated up the walls. But John heard no shouting or cheering

127

outside. It was uncannily quiet, and he went out to find out the cause of the silence.

The men stood thick; they had been stunned silent with disbelief. At the gates were two hundred Highlanders, the front rank kneeling. They had their muskets pointed towards the Yankees in such precision that not one barrel was an inch higher or lower than the next.

Captain Shortland stepped out of his office and bellowed an announcement through his cone: "Gentlemen, last night I ordered you to remain as you were until otherwise ordered. A rider has brought instructions that I am to keep you in prison. And that order, gentlemen, is not from my government but from your own government, your own States of America. Kindly return to your blocks immediately or the soldiers you see before you will be ordered to discharge their muskets into you."

"Nonsense, deuced nonsense! You are being detained in protective custody. Most of you have kinsfolk in England; all I need from those kinsfolk is a letter of authority guaranteeing shelter, and out you go through the gate. Or if any British or American ships need crew, give me a letter of authority and I'll give you the keys to the gate. I only need letters of authority. Your government's decision, Mr Adams. In the meantime, it's better to stay here where the men can be housed and fed and paid allowances until such time as your government can provide transport for home, eh? Makes sense, what?"

"Housed and fed and paid allowances," sneered John. "The men threw away their food and their money last night; they even threw the tools which made them money on the fire. We now depend on prison rations. We're back where we were three years ago. The suicides will start again."

"I'm genuinely sorry, but there's nothing I can do. Dammit, man, don't you think I want a letter of authority for myself from the Admiralty in London, giving me leave to quit this bloody castle of dungeons? Try your American agent. Oh, and we'll leave the gate open tonight. Nobody will break out, but it'll let the foxes in to clear up after the rats and ravens."

128

"Foxes with torches in their tails."

"A quotation, Mr Adams?" said Shortland, smiling.

"Cotton Mather."

"I'll bet he couldn't make tea half so good as you. Put the kettle on."

John was given no cause for hope by the American agent. Mr Beasley made a secret visit; he refused to see or be seen by the men, and talked only to John.

"You must remember, Mr Adams, that while you have been enjoying your daily markets and operas and such, your country has been fighting on its own soil for its very existence. It will take years and a great deal of money to put right the damage which has been done. How can the White House spare money to buy you tools for your own private gain in England?"

"Then take us home, and we'll use our skills to rebuild the United States."

"Our maritime losses were exceedingly heavy, and we have few ships left. But please assure the men, Mr Adams, that the New England forests are ringing to the woodman's axe, and that oak trees are being felled to build new ships. As soon as our government has these ships, you will be returned to our great and growing country."

"We don't have to wait for the acorns to grow?" asked John.

"Good day to you, sir."

When the news was given to the men, there was a riot. Two effigies were made, one labelled *Reuben Beasley*, the other *James Madison*. They were given a trial at which they were accused of betraying their countrymen and they were hanged. There was a general shout of "Burn the flag!" and a gang of men slowly swayed towards the main gate to pull down the Stars and Stripes.

Captain Shortland rushed into the yard and ordered a squad of Highlanders to protect the American flag. "Any man who causes wilful damage to His Majesty's property will be arrested and confined to the *cachot*!" he shouted.

"The American flag ain't His Majesty's property!" came a voice.

"No – but the flagpole is."

"Then give us the flag to burn, and King George can keep the flagpole and stick it up his royal arsehole.''

''I will convey your suggestion to His Majesty. In the meantime your flag will remain flying.''

The crowds burst out laughing, and the laughter echoed from the walls. The riot dispersed in good humour.

Later in the day, John heard an item of news which furthered the feeling of good humour.

Shortland sipped his tea and browsed through the London papers.

''By George, Mr Adams, listen to this. We may be at war with Cornwall any day, by the look of things.'' He laughed. ''It appears that some Cornishmen came up the Teign estuary, crept on board the ocean-going fishing fleet and sailed away with every vessel. 'An outrageous act of piracy,' says the paper. 'When the fishermen looked out upon the river one morning, their boats had gone, just disappeared. ''It is well known,'' said one of the fishing-boat skippers, ''that the Cornish folk is a nation of wreckers, and they have long been jealous of the Devonshire man's ability to sail across the Atlantic Ocean for good catches of cod.'' The Cornish man is not English,' it goes on, 'and is indeed more akin to the Frenchmen of Brittany. This is more than just an act of piracy, this is an act of war.' '' Shortland gave a loud laugh.

''Ah, but listen to this, Mr Adams. 'There was occasion for merriment in the court-house when one Mr Ernest Chapman, who had fished in the River Teign for over fifty years, was put up as a witness. He claimed he had fallen asleep in his small boat after an unprofitable evening spent awaiting the convenience of the salmon. He was awakened, he claimed, by the dipping of oars in water, and he saw many beautiful ladies rowing from the northern bank to the anchored ships. They were the most beautiful ladies he had ever seen, he told the court, and there were many of them. One of the ladies hoisted an ensign from the mast-head, and in the moonlight he could clearly see that it was the emblem of the serpent which tempted Eve. The vessels raised their anchors and drifted to sea on the ebb-tide. After Mr Chapman had been stood down, the magistrate announced that the Cornishmen would be apprehended and made to return the fishing-boats to the men of

130

Devonshire.' ''

But the news did not amuse the men.

"Ay, and them Cornish Yankee boys'll be back home kissing their wives and sweethearts; and where's us?"

"Yeah, and we gotta live like lice for ever and ever, cos we can't earn money no more."

"That's because you threw your wood and tools on the fire," said John.

"All right, Mr high-and-mighty Adams, get us our wood and tools back."

John called upon the Jew of Dartmoor. The old man was once again packing his goods and chattels. "So what are you asking me?" he said to John. "That I look up to the clouds and say 'O God of Abraham, send wood and woodworking tools down from the sky like you once sent manna to the children of Israel'?"

"Do you know where we could obtain these things?"

"Sure. I could get them for you in Exeter. But – " – he rubbed his finger in the palm of his other hand – "they will need the shekels, my friend."

John racked his brain to find ways of obtaining money; another opera, a Shakespeare play maybe, or write to the English and American newspapers. But any of these schemes would take months. He told Sally his problems.

"Problems?" she asked. "You've no problems. Here's the money." She emptied her jar of gold sovereigns. "Take what you want."

"I can't. It's your money. You may need it."

"Need it? Here on Dartmoor? Need money? Good morning, Mr Rabbit, I'll give you a golden guinea if you jump into my cauldron. Why, hello Mistress Salmon, here's the King's head if you will hop on my plate. I was thinking of making a necklace of these gold pieces, John. Take them, or I shall throw them in the bog."

She scooped the coins into her apron, and there was little doubt she would have done exactly what she said she'd do.

"We'll have to live on prison rations and government allowances for a few months," said John. "But it'll give the men some sort of hope again. And when you and I go to New England,

I shall – ''

"Of course you will, John my darling; you'll earn thousands and thousands of pounds."

"Dollars. We have dollars."

John handed the money over to the Jew of Dartmoor. "So you been talking to the God of Abraham," said the old Jew. "Some powerful prayer you must have used." He bit a coin. "Oh yes, this is manna. It has the taste."

The last day of the old year was a busy one. The Highlanders prepared for their important feast of Hogmanay; this consisted mainly of their stripping themselves naked, holding their noses and dipping down into vats of ice-cold water in order to be clean for the new year. As an extra cause for celebration, the Highlanders were informed they would be leaving Dartmoor in the morning. They were being sent to Europe under the command of the Duke of Wellington.

John was relieved that none of the Highlanders or Virginians wished to go back on their plans to change places. And as the Scotsmen felt more friendship towards the Americans than they did towards the English, he was reassured there would be no betrayals. He joined Sergeant Fraser and Ben Cotton in the alehouse.

"And remember," Ben Cotton warned the sergeant, "that you're a Virginian and no goddam Yankee. And one o' these days I'll be a meeting with you in Virginny, and maybe you and me can be off and chasing them buffalo together."

"Chasing?" asked the sergeant.

"Chasing is the word what I used. I usually chases a herd o' maybe five hundred . . ."

"On yer own, laddie?"

"No, I have a horse. And we corners 'em in a canyon, and I kills and skins 'em one by one. Often takes me half an hour. Course if there's maybe a thousand 'o them creatures, then 'tis like as not I'll be needing a partner just to keep me knife whetted."

Barely had John returned to the office and put the kettle on the fire when the sentry announced that two prisoners wished to see the captain. They were Big Dick and Deacon John. Again John had to take refuge behind an uplifted ledger, for he was always amused to bursting-point at the captain's complete lack of any sort of reaction whenever this couple confronted him. Whatever stupid requests these two Negroes made, Captain Shortland listened to them in all seriousness.

"With respect, sir," began Deacon John, "it has come to our intelligence that the Highland battalion is departing for Plymouth on the morrow. We humbly request that we may be permitted to accompany the aforesaid battalion in order that we may enrol in the King's Navy."

"Can't be done," said Shortland. "Part of the treaty and all that. No citizen of the States of America may henceforth be enlisted into the service of the British Navy. Sorry, gentlemen!"

"Ah, but sir, with the profoundest respect, we are slaves, and the United States has not seen fit to grant us nationality. We are, in their opinion, not Americans but black men. May I enquire therefore if black men are permitted to serve in your indefatigable navy?"

"Mmm," began Shortland, rubbing his chin in thought, "there have always been black men in our ships; some have served with distinction. But I must warn you that you'll be treated no better than bilge-rats. You'll be spat on, kicked and flogged."

"A most depressing thought, sir, if I may venture an opinion. But on the other hand, sir, if we are repatriated to America, we shall once again become slaves on the plantations, which was the reason for most of us escaping and signing up in Yankee ships in the first place. If, as you so charmingly put it, sir, we are spat upon, kicked by the boot, flogged by the lash, it will be a small price to pay for eventual freedom. His most gracious saintship Big Dick merely asks that after serving a few voyages on board one of King George's magnificent ships he may be deposited upon the sunny shores of Africa, where he will resume his regal position as emperor of that prolific continent."

Big Dick tossed his club into the hands of Deacon John, and clicked his hands and swayed his eyes.

"Moses and Jesus and Mr Noah come visit me up through de floor. Dey say I go to Africa shore where I be a slave no more. No baccy or cotton or chains of iron, live like king and eat like lion."

"I see your point," said Shortland. "Credentials will be written out, with instructions to disembark you both on African soil.''

"Er . . . no, sir,'' said Deacon John. "Not both of us. Only for His Imperial Omnipotence Big Dick. After my service I wish to be returned as a faithful retainer to His Grace the Duke of Kent.''

"Then you're under no obligation to serve in the King's Navy,'' said Shortland. "Good God, man, you're perfectly free to walk through the gate and resume service with the duke this very minute.''

"With respect, sir. The Angel Gabriel . . .''

"Da most angelest,'' grunted Big Dick.

"I stand corrected. The most angelest of Gabriels has insisted that I share the trials and tribulation of his dear friend on earth, Big Dick; that I assist him combat the devil and his evil ways, for it is reputed, sir, that the devil often goes to sea with the British Navy.''

"Oh, he does indeed,'' agreed the captain. "Very well, two recruitments for King George. You will leave with the battalion in the morning.''

"Nelson and Noah, Jonah and Jones, four fine sailors, rest der bones. De Lord send tempest and de Lord send gales, dis Big Dick gonna swaller dem whales.''

"Quite so,'' said the captain, and dismissed them with a flick of his fingers.

Big Dick snatched his club and did a shuffle dance out of the office. Deacon John bowed out backwards, raising and donning his top hat several times.

Shortland passed no comment about his visitors. He dipped his quill into the ink and began writing out their passports. Just once he looked up at his portrait and sighed.

The new year began with the firing of a cannon, and there were more cannons, and the prison bell began ringing and rang through most of the night, though it was often drowned by bagpipes. The deserting Highlanders refused to change their uniforms for prison yellow until one hour before parade, determined to remain Scotsmen until the last.

By nine o'clock they were in ranks, smart and clean, with the bayonets on their muskets flashing dazzlingly in the sunlight.

134

From outside came the beat of drums from the relieving regiment – no band, no music, just drums – and the new regiment marched in through the gate.

They carried their muskets at precisely the same angle, and their bayonets flashed in the sun. It was hypnotic. The men marched in perfect step, looking steadfastly to the front.

Captain Shortland conducted the necessary ceremonials for changing the guard and, as always, the new subalterns were dismissed and disappeared. The Highlanders sang their way out of the prison.

> "We twa hae paidl't i' the burn,
> Frae mornin sun till dine:
> But seas between us braid hae roar'd
> Sin' auld lang syne."

The Americans cheered the Highlanders; they were sorry to see them leave.

"And you may be sorry to see this new battalion arrive," Shortland told John. "It is the Forty-Ninth Foot, and has just returned from the Americas, where they took on the title of the Fighting Forty-Ninth. As far as I can gather, they were the only capable soldiers in the American war. They had a great victory at Queenstown Heights, where a thousand Americans were taken prisoner. But their commander, General Sir Isaac Brock, apparently held in great respect by them, had his head blown off by an American cannon in the battle. They've suffered dead and injured at the hands of your countrymen. What's more, they expected to be disbanded on return to England. Instead, they've been sent to Dartmoor. You will find them merciless and full of hate."

Shortlands's warning came true. The men in green were vindictive. They stood on the walls and jeered at the Yankees.

"Hey, you Yankee boys, you got some very willing women over there."

"Ay, willing and obliging. Very good at the bumps and bounces."

"Don't be surprised if y'aint got another little baby in the

135

family when y'gets home.''

"They ain't gonna get home. Didn't them women ask us to keep 'em here till they rots? They don't want you Yankee boys back, not after us. That's why you're being kept here.''

The Americans shuffled into their prison blocks, and the prison was as damp and as dreary as it had been years ago. The clouds overhead were heavy and full, it rained and rained, everything was damp and everything dripped.

There was nothing John could do. The Jew had disappeared from Princetown. No commodities arrived for which payment had been made. The friendly Highlanders had gone, and with them had gone Ben Cotton, even Big Dick and his assistant. His father had not replied to his letter; he felt he had no nationality, and that he was a cheat. Would George Washington have ridden away from Valley Forge each weekend for the comfort of a woman? What kind of little man was he?

"I belong to no country," he told Sally.

"That's right, you belong to me. And I belong to no country," she said, and that was the kind of answer he expected from her.

"But I'm cheating on my Americans, and I'm even cheating on the English.''

"I've made a fortune by cheating on the English, so don't worry about the English, for the English can take care of themselves.''

"It's mainly my own men. I hear them groaning at night for want of a woman. Sometimes I feel I could organise them, and lead them to overpower the soldiers, and march them away.''

"Where to?''

"God knows! Just march away to nowhere!''

"And leave me?''

"Ay, there's the rub: you are holding me on the moor, and I'm a willing captive. I'll never leave you! But my men have to return to their wives and maidens. Sally, it's three years!''

"Have you forgotten? It's you who are keeping me a captive on the moor. Besides, the bailiff's daughter of Islington waited seven long years. Your men have only to wait for ships.''

"Yes, and for how long? They'll put commerce before repatriation.''

"John, don't worry!''

It was easy for him to forget his worries when he looked at her. The slight, ever so slight, twist on her knee gave her almost a limp and made her appear vulnerable, which of course she wasn't, but that didn't matter. She was like a damsel in distress who had been wounded by an evil dragon – perhaps the sulphurous fire from its nostrils had slightly scorched her knee. That was nonsense, yet he felt the need to protect her, to poise his lance on her behalf. But he knew that the truth like the boot was on the other leg. Yet again it was her eyes, which although more often than not were wide and gave the impression of surprise, could narrow themselves and give the feeling of timidity, helplessness, begging for care and tenderness. Her eyes always looked straight at him; she rarely looked away. Her nose was imperceptibly turned up, causing a casual imperfection that enhanced her beauty. And her hair, though cut short, made perfect waves on her neck, like the natural undulations of waves on the sea-shore. Her lips were usually slightly parted, showing a thin line of white teeth; it was as though she were about to say something. When John told her, he asked her what it was she would say.

"I'm always about to say 'John. Oh, John'," she said.

"Sally!"

They sank down together on the bed. She had never been so tender or caring towards him, even during the season of the wasps. She stroked his forehead and the back of his neck. She gasped and moaned with sweet love.

Afterwards, she filled his tobacco pipe, and she began cooking the tastiest-smelling meal while singing the sweetest of songs.

"Tell me more about your bright and shining New England?" she asked.

"It's only a small part of America," said John. And America is a country without an end. There are waterfalls higher than the clouds, and always wearing rainbows, and lakes which are seas of themselves, wider than from here to France. You can ride in a straight line over the wilderness for weeks. And the Mississippi River is as wide as London town, and that's where we'll go, across the Mississippi. That's Lyonesse for you, darling."

"Have you seen all this?"

"No – but I've heard. And there are Red Indian tribes with

names like Huron, Cheyenne, Delaware, Chicasaw, Shawnee, Dakota and Mohawk. And they have a religion which probably you would understand.''

"Have you seen them?''

"A few. But I've heard of the others. Don't they sound better than your tin men and copper men and mundic men?''

"I'd love to see them.''

"And there are animals you've never seen before. Bears . . .''

"I've seen them dancing in chains at Exeter.''

"Here they have no chains.''

"Go on!''

"And wolves, beavers, racoons and buffalo. And there are whippoorwills and snow-geese.''

"I'd love to cook them for you, darling.''

John laughed. "Yes, if I could catch them.''

"Oh, you'd catch 'em, John.'' She pretended to be thinking things out. "Let's see, what shall we have for our evening meal? Ah yes, there's six buffaloes you shot; we'll have those with mushrooms. But first, racoon soup. Did you like those beavers we had for lunch? I'd like to cook you them snow-geese, but there isn't any snow to cook 'em in.''

They both laughed, and for a time John felt better. But his depression came back, although it was not as strong as it had been; it was more of a grumbling depression.

"I still think I'm worse than useless; I'm a damned cheat; I'm not doing a blessed thing for my men!''

"Oh, isn't he full of pity for himself!'' said Sally. "Let me see, didn't you tell me you'd been to a college?''

"Harvard.''

"And they gave you a brand-new, sparkling brain?''

"Just a little second-hand one.''

"Never mind. And aren't you using it on behalf of your Yankees? Haven't you got them a school, a college, a coffee-house, an orchestra, and books, books, books by the dozen?''

"I suppose so!''

"He supposes so. And was that achieved by a bayonet or a brain? A brain. Your brain. Did you want to be a hero, then? A mighty warrior? A knight at arms? Oh John, you're using your

138

brain, and that's enough. Why must you be a hero?"

"I guess every man would like to be a hero, and then he knows he's a man."

"Oh, you're a man all right! And you're my man. When we cross that Mississippi of yours, I'll be quite content as long as you keep me supplied with six buffaloes a day for eating purposes, and racoons for roasting, and chicsaws for a pudding, and whippoorwills . . ."

"They sing all night."

"What do? Buffaloes?"

John put his fingers to his head as mock horns, and went 'moo' and charged at her.

> "Youth's the season made for joys,
> Love is then our duty.
> She alone who that employs
> Well deserves her beauty."

CHAPTER NINE

Teeth of the Furious Tygers

There's a lonely prison a mile from hell
Wherein six thousand Yankees dwell;
They rob and cheat and fight and lie;
Ain't nothing for them to do but die.

Prison songs filled the prison blocks at night. The men felt sorry for themselves; they were becoming resigned to a perpetual incarceration. The redcoats jeered them, and repeatedly recited, with just a few changes, William Cowper's popular poem about John Gilpin, a citizen of credit and renown, whose horse ran away with him:

"Away went Madison, and away
Went Madison's hat and wig:
He lost them sooner than at first,
For why? – they were too big."

But the Americans were so low in spirit that they hardly noticed the insults any more. They shuffled in circles around the prison yards; they ate their rations without conversation; their tradesmen no longer called out their wares, for there were no wares; the boys didn't turn up for school; the college was unattended. There was no point in learning to become good Americans if America had left them as castaways in a grim prison. They couldn't even escape by joining the British Navy, for the British Navy no longer needed them, and was bound by the treaty not to press them.

James Ludlow of Greenfield, Connecticut, committed suicide, and Christopher Hubbard of Baltimore, Maryland, committed suicide, and William Allen of Andover, Massachusetts, committed suicide; there was nothing else worth doing. 'Tom Bowling' became the burial song. The Forty-Ninth played no music, but every night they beat upon the drums, and the drum beats vibrated in the ears of the prisoners; there was no place in the prison where the drums could not be heard.

John Adams knew he would have to postpone the chicasaws, racoons and snow-geese. He couldn't desert his countrymen; he had to do what he could for them. He advertised in the London newspapers for American skippers to take on able-bodied mariners, and he wrote letters for men who had kinsfolk in England. When a crew was required, he always included one boy and one Highlander, for the Highlanders would be shot if they were discovered as deserters. He also placed Negroes in his selection, but only in ships bound for the ports of northern states.

When he had abandoned hope of the Jew, two carts arrived at the prison. They contained wood and brand-new, sparkling tools of the finest quality. Along with them came the old Jew himself. He was dressed in a long black coat down to his ankles and a shiny top hat which, when he removed it in salutation to John, revealed a beautifully embroidered skull-cap on the back of his bushy head.

"So the God of Abraham has been good to this poor Hebrew?" began the Jew. "With the manna you gave me, I bought the timber merchant's business. Good, eh? So I now repay you with a fair interest."

In twos and threes the men drifted back to their benches. They had lost interest in the ships, and John advised them to make furniture in the Chippendale, Hepplewhite and Sheraton fashion, because, he pointed out, immigrants to the United States would not bring chairs with them whatever else they brought. He also encouraged them to construct the cotton and wool frames of Kay, Hargreaves, Arkwright and Crompton, because, he told them, the new America should never become dependent upon old Europe again. The men did what he asked, but with very little heart.

And then Captain Shortland came up with some news.

"You may be interested to learn, Mr Adams, that the British Army in North America has suffered a major defeat."

"What?"

141

"Massacred at New Orleans by a General Jackson with militiamen from Kentucky and Tennessee."

"Turkey shooters, bear hunters and Indian fighters."

"General Sir Edward Pakenham and all his officers were slaughtered at the head of their troops. And all this while *Favourite* was fast approaching America with the peace treaty. I imagine the stolen victory has just about saved Madison's neck. Bad luck, eh?"

"No, sir! Good luck! Wheeeeeee!" shouted John, doing a bit of a dance with unrestrained delight.

"Really, Mr Adams! Such an uncharitable display!"

"No, sir! New Orleans! We were brought up in Agincourt. We're the same stock."

"More's the pity," grunted the captain. "Why weren't General Jackson and his Kentucky men in Europe facing Napoleon?"

"It's at moments like this that a cup of tea is called for," said John, reaching for the kettle.

"Oh, there's one more little item." Shortland handed John several sheets of words and music. "It seems your country has a national song. One of the subalterns brought it back with him. Somebody called Scott Keys was being held on a British ship while they bombarded a fortress outside Baltimore. He no doubt borrowed an English pen and used English ink with which to write it."

"Thank you, sir. Unfortunately our orchestra is unable to read music."

"I'm afraid you'll get no help from the Forty-Ninth. All they can do is bang drums."

John spread the news of New Orleans, and he had the words of the new song printed on broadsheets. The men tried all sorts of tunes to the words, including all the tunes from *The Beggar's Opera*, but none of them fitted. It was agreed they would face the flag every morning and recite the first verse. The men recovered some of their identity; they became more cheerful; they started cutting and carving the wood with professional pride. When the redcoats shouted 'John Gilpin' at them, they hurled 'Andrew Jackson' back in their faces.

The uplift didn't last too long. News came that Napoleon had escaped exile on Elba and was hell-bent on raising a world-conquering army. The wars would never end.

And then Africa fever broke out, and once more men began to die in the hospital with screaming hallucinations.

The artist, John Atkinson, continued to paint, but his work changed; the reds and yellows disappeared; his work became that of a frightful genius. All his paintings were now of Dartmoor Prison with heaped and unreal clouds above it, and evil threatening tors surrounding it. Those who looked at his work felt that their eyes had been put out, their tongues torn away, their aching bodies chained inside the painted prison blocks. Men shunned the pictures.

"I start to paint the green banks and yellow flowers along the Hudson," he told John, "but my brush takes over and dips into the black and red."

One night Atkinson walked out through the gate. Nobody, not even the sentries, tried to stop him. Good riddance of an evil painter, who, it was thought by many, would one day paint their souls and sell the pictures to the devil.

A week later his dead, twisted body was discovered and brought back to the prison in a cart.

Captain Shortland refused to allow anybody to see the corpse except John Adams, Dr McGrath and Charles Andrews. The eyes were wide – wide open and staring, the mouth was one half smile, one half frown, there was a smell of burning. The sight of the body would have terrified both prisoners and guards.

"This man has come to his death through no human agency," said Captain Shortland.

Dr. McGrath was inclined to disagree, but he admitted he had never seen a body so diabolically contorted.

"The old dragon underground," said John.

"And that's nonsense," said the doctor. "There's a scientific explanation."

"I agree," said John, "and with Captain Shortland's permission, I'd like to take Dr McGrath, Mr Andrews and an escort of soldiers on an experimental expedition."

"And what is it we'll be looking for, would ye tell me?" asked the doctor. "Is it the banshee?"

"We've got to discover the cause of death."

"That I can't deny."

"There must be a logical reason, though I must admit I no longer know the logical from the illogical."

"Who does after a year on the moor?" added Shortland. "Take your escort and bring the devil back in chains."

The body had been found face down in a stream to the south of Fox Tor. The head had been pointing downstream. John kicked and splashed through the water upstream in an attempt to retrace Atkinson's route. He suddenly yelled for the doctor to join him.

Half-way up a bank, and hidden by gorse bushes, was a small cave opening not unlike the entrance to a kiln. There was a heap of small rocks scattered nearby. The doctor crawled inside, being warned by John to take great care.

Within seconds he had scrambled back out, wincing and shaking his fingers as though they'd been burned. "Ah now, and would ye be knowing something?" said the doctor. He put the tip of his finger to his tongue, then spat out; then he rushed to the stream and rinsed his hands.

"The dragon underground?" said John.

"Ye could say that, indeed ye could. For 'tis thick with arsenic in there. The walls are coated with it. And there is a kind of boiler, as though someone had been boiling rocks. Now isn't that the very thing, Mr Adams? The poor lost soul discovered there was a hot fire in the cave, and he wriggled his way in to get warm and dry. Sure, maybe his mind was a touch distraught, but in he went, and fell asleep with exhaustion and that, and him breathing in the steam all the time. Then he felt the agony of the poison within himself and crawled out for air. And sure did he run down to the bloody stream, screaming and yelling, till he dropped dead with convulsions. Come to think of it, he had the features of a man who'd died in torture with arsenic poisoning, but 'twas the last thing I'd be looking for."

"Mundic," said John. "And that's what killed all the others."

"What?"

"Mundic. That's what they call it on the moor."

"'Tis iron pyrites, y'mean."

144

"Maybe."

"And that's how the others died. A dragon, did ye say? Me boy, ye've killed a dragon, so ye have."

John thought of the grotesque dwarf he had frightened away, and felt warm from his love for Sally; she had fed the twisted man like a child feeds a swan. She had compassion, whereas he was self-centred.

The news of the mundic did not please the Americans. They had built a church with their toil and sweat, a church to pray in, and they'd been brought up to believe that the way to combat the devil was with prayer; but here the devil was using science, and they felt that prayer alone was not sufficient to stand up to science.

"We built a church for parson Nick
Who takes our souls with arsenic."

Similar heavy songs were chanted in the Negro block, for since Big Dick had joined the King's Navy they had been left without a leader and had become broken human beings again.

"Dey sold ma lovely Hannah
To a slave boss in Savannah,
Ain't got no wife no more."

One man would chant such words out loud, and the rest of the block would take up the dirge:

"Sat on ma daddy's knee
Till dey hanged him from a tree,
Ain't got no daddy no more."

And throughout these heavy songs, which got lower and lower, the drums of the Forty-Ninth rattled and vibrated through the rain.

There were several deaths from African fever, after which panic started and murders began. These usually happened after John had selected a crew for a ship's master. One of the men picked for the draft would be found with his throat cut and the murderer

145

would take his place, threatening the same fate to any of the draft who betrayed him. But the draft usually had the courage to denounce the murderer, especially after one or two of these killers were condemned by the cell block, and were branded M and then hanged from a beam.

Executions became necessary amongst the British guards. Strengthened by the discovery that there wasn't a fiend on the moor, only dangerous man-made caves, and frightened that the African fever would become an epidemic and annihilate the whole complement of the prison, Americans and British, there were desertions, in ones, twos and threes. The deserters were usually caught, and condemned by their own officers to be shot before a firing-squad. Every man jack behind the granite walls lived in fear, the British perhaps more than the Americans because they were vastly outnumbered.

The only minute of humour for John in the four months since the peace treaty came was when Blowzy Bet applied for a passport of release.

"Oh, good morning, sweetheart, sir!" said Bet to the captain, giving him a playful tap on the shoulder. There wasn't even the twitch of an expression on Shortland's face, and once again John had to take refuge behind a ledger.

"What is it?" snapped Shortland.

"I have here a letter, thanks to Mr Adams who is a real primrose, from Mr Edmund Kean offering me a position of employment at the Drury Lane Theatre."

"What as? Doll Tearsheet or Cleopatra?"

"Oh, you silly little magnolia blossom, you. Course not. As costume and make-up, dear."

Shortland snatched the letter and read it. "You can leave on the next detail. And put some trousers on before you leave the prison."

"Oh, sir, you're most impudent," said Bet, and he wiggled goodbye wth two fingers, and turning to John said: "Goodbye, plum."

Shortland looked up at his portrait for a second. "Write his passport out and I'll sign it, plum!"

Men approached John with offers of bribes for him to put them

146

on the next draft and Richard Webber of Kennebunk, Maine, offered him a thousand pounds, which had been his prize-money during service with the British Navy, but John refused all bribes. So the death threats came. So many death threats he was convinced somebody would take a thrust at him. He surprised himself by not caring about the threats to his life. Years ago, death was something terrible and sacred; now it was as commonplace as a sneeze. Death was a permanent resident in Dartmoor Prison.

And the music of death seemed to be the drums of the Forty-Ninth. They tattooed and rat-a-tat tattooed, and many times each night the redcoats sang:

"Whene'er we are commanded to storm the palisades,
 Our leaders march with fusees, and we with hand grenades;
 We throw them from the glacis about the enemies' ears,
 Sing tow, row, row, row, row, row, for the British
     Grenadiers."

The Americans, who now outnumbered their guards by six to one, could easily have overwhelmed them with song, and would have given their right arms to do so. Indeed, their new song had threats of retaliation with the rockets' red glare and bombs bursting in air, but they'd no tune to sing it to, and without a tune they were defeated.

The months passed and the days got longer and warmer. On the Friday afternoon when John rode to Sally's cottage it was nearing the summer solstice, and the longest day. It wouldn't get dark, really dark, until approaching eleven o'clock. John took a deep breath of the wine-rich heather air; it was the air of freedom, and death was left languishing in prison; here was life and life was precious, and Sally was precious.

"I'm glad you came early, cos there's a little trip I want to take you on," she said.

"Where?"

"Ah, just you see."

"What about food?"

"We can eat and drink at a tavern. How's that? Better than my

147

cooking, eh? Venison and old ale, which I can't supply you with.
Or maybe artichokes and French wine, after you've seen what I'm
going to show you. Allons-y!''

She heeled her horse to speed, and John had no alternative but
to follow. Across the moor they galloped, keeping to no path but
relying on Sally's sideways glances at the tors, until they came to
the ruins of Buckfast Abbey and stopped to give their horses a
drink by the River Dart.

"I bet 'tis crammed full o' ghosts of monks and the like," said
Sally. "And all a-counting their beads with skeletons hands, and
a-singing their 'Ave marias' from silent skulls. But we gotta move
on, so giddy-up there!''

The next stop was at the base of a steep, heavily wooded but
eerie hill, steep like the sides of an upturned bucket, and on the
top of which were more gloomy ruins.

"But this be the spot for real ghosties, John. 'Tis Berry
Pomeroy, and there's three of 'em, all ladies and all very
beautiful, and one of 'em's a real fair enchantress. 'Tis said she
was walled up in a dark dungeon till she died of starvation and
that her ghost walks the ramparts, and if you look upon her fairy
face, you'll surely die very soon.''

"How can anybody ever know unless they've died? Nonsense!''

"All right, just you look up to the top of the ruins and shout
'Jane!'.''

"Was that her name?''

"I dunno, but I reckon she might answer to it. Go on now!''

"No, because it's silly." But he was afraid to look up through
the trees.

"Kiss me, John!''

"Not here.''

"Why not?''

"It's the wrong time and place.''

"Are you afraid you'll go back to the days of old and open your
eyes to a fairy face?''

"No, I'm not!''

"Well, kiss me!''

He kissed her with his eyes wide open, and it was a very quick
kiss.

"If that's a kiss, 'tain't worth bothering about." She laughed.

"Is this the trip which was so pressing? To gallop around the countryside on a tour of haunted ruins?"

"No, me dear! I said artichokes and wine, remember? Come on, then! Don't you be bothered with them ghost stories."

They rode through green countryside. The fields were covered in white and yellow flowers, the chestnut trees had large, cream-coloured blossoms and the air seemed as thick and as soothing as cream itself. They trotted into a small fishing village called Tor Quay, and here it was like a foreign carnival; everything was hustle and bustle. There were stagecoaches from London and Bristol, some coming, some leaving. There were gentlemen in top hats, ladies with parasols and fans, all chattering excitedly, all laughing. Down at the quayside, many fishing-boats were clustered together and bobbing up and down like ducklings at duckling time, and the fishermen were shouting: "Come now, ladies and gentlemen, give a bob to see his nob!" "Only a shilling! The King's head to see an emperor!"

> "Cock-a-doodle-doo! Fresh from Waterloo!
> Napoleon is seen without his Josephine,
> Beneath our British banners,
> And for only two tanners."

> "Come and see Emperor Boneypart
> What cracked his head on the stony part."

The crowds of ladies and gentlemen were stepping on gang planks and crowding on to the fishing-boats. A man selling small French tricolours was doing a brisk trade. Sally stepped on to a gang plank of a boat called *The Dragonfly*, and John followed her. She paid two shillings.

"What's it all about?" asked John.

"We're going to see Napoleon. He's on board the British ship out there. He stands on deck most of the day being painted by a painter. And he's in full-dress. He sometimes smiles, they say. Worth two shillings, isn't it, John?"

"I suppose so." Inwardly, John was quite thrilled at the

149

prospect.

"Something to tell our children, eh?" She put her arm round him and squeezed him.

The fishing-boat approached HMS *Bellerophon* and they could see Napoleon standing on deck. He was in uniform and wore all his decorations and a sash; he looked a proud man, not too unhappy. Sally was very excited. As *The Dragonfly* neared *Bellerophon* she waved her tricolour and cheered "Vive la France! Vive la République! Vive le Grand Empereur!" For a brief moment Napoleon smiled at her. She leaned back on John. "Oh John, I feel giddy! He smiled at me!"

The bay was filled with crowded fishing-boats, and dozens of people cheered Napoleon as their vessels touched *Bellerophon*. Giving it a kiss, as the boat skippers called it. John remembered the letter from his father wherein he'd described the Bostonians cheering a British ship with a British flag which had just vanquished an American one. The world could turn itself upside-down at the drop of a hat. As the vessel headed back towards the shore, John was able to appreciate what a beautiful coastline it was, with its red cliffs and green curls.

Sally was still breathless when they set foot on shore. "Quel jour! C'est bon, c'est magnifique! Mais, oh mon pauvre! C'est le commencement de la fin! John, I must have a brandy, and you must have the ale of old England and a haunch of venison – a Robin Hood meal."

They untethered their horses and she led him to another fishing village called Brixham, and to an inn half-way up a cliff road, from where they could see the white *Bellerophon* in the golden sunset.

When they had finished their meal, and only a lantern dot was left of the ship, John sprawled with his legs out and lit his pipe. "I suppose it's English humour to place Napoleon aboard a ship called *Bellerophon*. Bellerophon was a Greek hero who tamed the flying horse Pegasus and thus was able to slay the fire-breathing monster Chimaera."

"Napoleon is not Kym. . .what you said. He's not a fire-breathing monster anyhow."

"The English seem to think he was. I'm only telling you the

myth.''

Sally clutched John's arm and looked earnestly at him. "Have you finished? Can we ride? Let's go home!"

"But . . ."

"Never mind 'but', John. Let's ride."

They left the warmth and the light of the inn and galloped away. Instinctively, Sally knew her way home in the darkness. There was a moon, but not enough to show up the tors.

Inside the cottage, she grabbed him by both arms and looked straight in his eyes. "John, you said you'd do anything for me?"

"Yes."

"And that you wanted to be a hero to prove to yourself that you're a man?"

"Well, yes."

"Now's your chance! Capture Napoleon!"

"What!"

"Capture Napoleon! It's easy. Look, I know a woman who knows the painter, and the captain of the *Elephant*. . ."

"*Bellerophon*," corrected John.

"No matter – that ship . . . the captain told the painter he'd have to finish the painting in three days. So you've got three days."

"Hold on! I've got nothing at all."

"Three days. And you've got thousands of Yankees in the prison who are armed and could break out. You told me yourself. How long would it take them to march on Tor Quay? A handful of miles."

"Some of them would get killed."

"Some of them are already committing suicide, like you said. Which is the best way to go?"

"And when we get to Tor Quay?"

"John, use your loaf! If you get there after midnight, all those fishing-boats will be lying idle after a day spent ferrying sightseers, and their crews would be in the tavern. Most of your men are sailors, and you'd make a Yankee armada. You could sweep aboard *Elephant* . . ."

"*Bellerophon*."

"Well, correct me: but you could swoop on the ship like foxes

151

on an old hen. Just one unsupported warship in the bay, and the most famous man in the world a prisoner on board. It'd be like taking candy from a child.''

John remembered the story of how John Paul Jones with four and twenty ragtag and bobtail Marines from the *Ranger* had overcome a hundred sleeping redcoats and captured Whitehaven without a struggle, without a casualty. He was tempted. It was a daring plan. ''But no!'' he said.

''No? How can you say no? It could work. The English don't seem to realise that not so many miles from their star prisoner is what amounts to an American fortress. It could be their one great blunder in this campaign.''

John thought of his country's history. How forty years ago a handful of amateur colonials had taken on the greatest army in the world; how only six months ago Andrew Jackson had decimated some British regiments.

''But no!''

''Why do you keep saying 'But no'?''

''My country and England are not at war. I'd be a traitor to peace. This time Britain could throw everything they'd got at us, and I doubt if we'd survive.''

''Not if you took Napoleon across to Le Havre, which is only eighty miles from Tor Quay. He's still their national hero, second only to Joan of Arc. They'd rally to him once more, and England would have its hands full. You'd change history!''

''We're not at war.''

''You've said that. All right, you're not at war, but the English still hold your ships. They're blaming the Americans for not supplying transport for repatriation, but they've only to give you your own ships back. Take Napoleon for a hostage, then. But take the ship – it's yours for the taking!''

''I can't! I won't be responsible for a war or bloodshed. You said yourself Harvard gave me a brain; well, that brain tells me no, and I've got to listen to it.''

Sally flung herself on the bed and began crying, sobbing, shaking. ''It was a clever plan,'' she blubbered.

''It was a very clever plan,'' soothed John. ''And I'm glad you took me to see Napoleon, but'' – he shrugged his shoulders –

152

"I don't want to let loose the dogs of war."

He bent over her to stroke her, but she brushed him aside. "Go away! Get out of my sight! I hate you! You're a coward!" John pleaded with her, but she remained obstinate. She sat up: "Why are you in my cottage? I don't want you in my home! Get out of here!"

It was the grey of early daylight. John led his horse slowly. He hoped she would call him back; she didn't. He swung on to the horse's back and rode like the wings of the morning. He reached Princetown at first cock-crow.

That same morning, a bright young peacock of an officer sauntered into the office to announce quite casually that the depot had run completely out of flour. There was no bread either for prisoners or soldiers.

"Good God, man!" exploded Shortland. "You officers are so busy rolling dice like the fifteenth sons of fifteen earls, and your men are so occupied banging drums like children with toys, that you've failed to notice we're running out of provisions. You're not supplying delicious dainties for half a dozen jolly fellows at Eton – you're victualling seven thousand crazy men cooped up in a moorland prison."

"Terribly sorry, sir! With permission, I'll take a troop of soldiers and six wagons to Plymouth for supplies."

"Over my dead body, sir. Once you and your troops reach the Plymouth whorehouses we'll be lucky to see you this side of Christmas. I shall take the troop and the wagons. Have them ready in fifteen minutes."

"Yes, sir!" The peacock ambled out.

"Mr Adams, open up the provisions store and distribute the ship's biscuits. If they can't eat them, they can repair their boots with them. Apologise and try to explain to the men what happened. I shall return tomorrow."

Inside fifteen minutes, the train of wagons rumbled out through the gate. Almost immediately there were cries for bread. Rumour had it that Captain Shortland had abandoned the prison because of the epidemics of African fever and lung diseases; it was spread around that he had left them to die of starvation. Men began pulling down the walls. Holes were made in the ammunition store and muskets handed from hand to hand. Soldiers who tried to stop them were stoned. A number had to be taken to hospital.

John locked himself in the office overnight. He feared the Americans would see him as a traitor, the British as a Yankee ringleader; in any case, the office was the heart of the prison, and it seemed only right that a few lanterns should remain alight in it. Fires were started down below in the yards, and there was spasmodic musket fire, but, worst of all, the drums of hell started up and vibrated through the night.

Shortly after first light, the Americans grouped with the intention of breaking down the main gate. The soldiers disappeared completely; there was neither the rattle of a musket nor the glint of a bayonet. Dartmoor Prison belonged to the Americans. They marched towards the main gate, but suddenly they stopped in their tracks, for the gate opened and Captain Shortland rode in, followed by his troop of soldiers and six loaded provision wagons.

He looked around at the debris. "Clean this mess up!" he ordered. "And rebuild this wall!" The Americans refused, and he detailed soldiers who were off duty.

There was a general feeling of victory amongst the Yankees. They hopped, skipped and jumped, and a game of rounders was begun. The idea seemed to be to hit the ball towards the soldiers who were rebuilding the wall. The ball-throwers had never pitched so strong, the hitters had never hit so hard, and the cheerers had never cheered so loud. The sunlight lit the walls up red.

The best striker by far was Henry Frelitch of Liverpool, Pennsylvania; and the best pitcher within ten thousand miles was Josiah Gun of Salem. Every time he struck with his bat, Frelitch managed to run the four posts, and the spectators were so busy shading their eyes with their hands to watch the ball soaring up and up that occasionally he was able to cheat and cut diagonally back to the first post. Josiah Gun spat on the ball and juggled it and rubbed it between the palms of his hands in an attempt to

154

put magic into it, and he aimed it faster than a cannon-ball, but the 'plock' from Frelitch's bat always told that the little ball had been punished severely.

Henry Frelitch stood feet astride, the bat poised above his shoulders ready to swipe.

> "I'm going to hit the ball
> Clear over the wall,
> And I ain't going to see where it will fall."

Josiah Gun pitched. Clorrup! The ball soared like a pheasant over the high wall.

The redcoats on the ramparts had been sneering at the Yankees, yelling that it was a game played by little girls in England, when the ball soared over their heads.

"Please, can we have our ball back?"

The ball had landed in the market yard, which was the first yard leading to the main gate, and it had been kept locked until the hole in the wall was repaired.

"Can't understand Yankee talk," shouted a sentry. "You'll have to speak in English, and ask nicely."

Captain Shortland and John had been watching the game through the office window, Shortland as usual twiddling his fingers behind his back and rocking on his feet. "Oh, for God's sake give them their bloody ball back!" he said under his breath.

"We want our ball!" came the cry from several hundred men.

"I think they're saying they've got no balls!" Shouted a sentry to another soldier further down the ramparts.

"Ay, that's what their womenfolk say about them too!" The soldier yelled back.

There was a sudden wave of prisoners towards the yard gate. They began thumping at the gate and heaving at it to break it.

"You have my permission to join your countrymen immediately," Shortland snapped at John.

John was instinctively aware that this was a command he dare not question. "Yes sir."

Shortland ordered his sentry to call out the guard on the bugle and have the prison alarm bell rung. John rushed down the steps

155

and joined the crowd below. They had already cracked the yard gate.

"Let's have their balls!" shouted one of the prisoners.

"Like we did at New Orleans!" shouted another.

"Let's take the prison!"

"Ay, lads, let's take the prison!"

The gate fell, and a thousand men streamed through it. John was carried along with them. Fifty soldiers were running to take up their lines in front of the main gate.

Captain Shortland walked across the yard. He picked up the ball and handed it to Josiah Gun. "Your ball, sir, and better luck next throw." He walked towards the line of soldiers and addressed the sergeant: "Where are your officers?"

"We only got two and an ensign, sir. And they're having dinner, sir."

"Then we mustn't give them indigestion by disturbing them. Have fifteen men load their muskets. The remainder to stand away." Shortland shouted through his cone: "Gentlemen, I would request you to return to your blocks."

"And a pig's arse!" shouted a voice. "We've had enough! We're taking over the prison!"

There was a roar of approval.

"Gentlemen," bellowed Shortland, "in pursuance of the Riot Act, I, Captain Thomas Shortland, being an officer of His Majesty's Navy, do proclaim this to be an unlawful assembly with the purpose of bringing about violence. I order you to disperse immediately."

"Lay down your arms, captain!" came a voice.

The crowd pushed forward, and John found himself being hustled to the front rank.

"Come on, Adams. Take over!"

"Aye!" shouted the mob.

"Discharge your muskets over their heads!" ordered Shortland.

The fifteen soldiers raised their muskets as one man. Click – clack! Crack! A volley of shot splattered above the heads of the prisoners. The crack echoed and re-echoed around the walls.

"They can't shoot straight! Come on, lads – we've got 'em!" shouted Josiah Gun.

156

Rocks were thrown at the soldiers.

"I'm ordering you to disperse!" shouted Shortland.

The men continued to rush forward.

"We're free men. We're at peace. You've no authority to keep us here."

"Ay, down with the main gate!"

"I have the authority of your government and King George's government."

"Sod King George!"

"Discharge your muskets into the rioters!" ordered Captain Shortland. There was a little hesitancy among the fifteen men, no doubt because they knew the rioters had some guns. Shortland grabbed a musket from one of the men and levelled it at the mob. "Any soldier who doesn't shoot when I shoot, will be shot himself." He discharged his musket, and the men did likewise. There was a succession of cracks.

John was hit in the arm. In a split second, it seemed to John that the shot had come from Shortland's musket. The pain burned, and his left arm dropped limp. Blood splashed into his face from the man next to him. There were groans and yells, and men dropped dead and wounded. John sank to his knees, holding his arm. The squad unsheathed their bayonets and fixed them.

"I did not order you to fix bayonets!" yelled Shortland.

But all was now out of hand. Most of the prisoners fought each other to back away, but the men behind them were still pushing ahead. More and more rocks fell on the soldiers, and there was occasional musket fire from some of the prisoners at the far rear. The soldiers advanced with their bayonets, jabbing as they went. There were more yells and screams as men was slashed by bayonets. Prisoners and soldiers were too close for further shooting and engaged in hand-to-hand fighting. Slowly the wave of men was pushed back. Guards on the ramparts began shooting indiscriminately. The crowd dispersed into groups, and the groups shuffled towards their own prison blocks. The redcoats still prodded them with their bayonets as the men pushed and kicked each other to get through the doors to safety.

John Adams looked around the yard. It was almost empty but for dead and badly wounded men lying still in pools of blood. Just a few feet away from him was the rounders ball.

Dr McGrath and Charles Andrews and other hospital crews rushed into the yard to remove the bodies.

"That was wilful murder, Captain Shortland!" said Dr McGrath. "Sure the devil got into ye!"

Charles Andrews spat on the captain's uniform. "You're a fiend! You're a butcher!" he screamed.

"Do your best for the injured, doctor," said Shortland, and he left the yard.

The sergeant ordered his troop back into ranks and marched them away.

For the first time since the block had been occupied by prisoners, the doors were bolted. There were no drum tattoos that night. The shot had not entered John's arm; it had merely ripped a piece of flesh away. His wound was thickly bandaged and his arm put in a sling.

The hospital was a sight and sound of carnage. In addition to the casualties there were the men who were ill with the African fever and chest diseases. Throughout the night there was coughing and spitting and groaning, and from time to time the unearthly scream of a man who was having a limb sawn off. Dr McGrath and Andrews were themselves covered in blood. Sometimes they threw buckets of water over each other to wash themselves down and keep themselves awake. Medical assistants went from man to man issuing large tankards of rum and brandy and any other form of alcohol they could find. Towards morning light the groans had subsided a little. John closed his eyes and listened to limbs being amputated. His stomach turned each time he heard the thud of a severed limb drop on the floor. He took stock. Nine men had been killed and thirty-eight seriously wounded; nineteen others slightly wounded. Dr McGrath and Charles Andrews had conducted nine amputations during the night.

John walked out into the yard. It was warm and sunny. There was no smell of breakfast being cooked from either the prison cookhouse or the barracks. Doors were unbolted, but no prisoner showed his face.

On a bugle call, the entire battalion of redcoats mustered in the yards, and once more the frightening drums began to vibrate.

158

Officers, still buttoning their tunics, took up parade positions. The drums stopped. Approaching was the sound of a brass band. The gate opened and a new battalion almost jogged and danced in to the tune of 'Dashing Away with the Smoothing Iron'.

After the normal changing the guard ceremonies, the drums of the Forty-Ninth passed under the archway and the men marched away. John learned that the new garrison was the Somersetshire Militia. They were jolly men from the neighbouring county, and it was clear they were more used to bearing barley than carrying muskets, for their muskets were slung over their shoulders at all angles, like pins in a pincushion. The prisoners came out of their doors, and some of the Somersetshire men waved hello to them. They seemed unable to march in step. John remembered they were from the country of his ancestors.

John assumed he should report for duty. More than ever, some sort of liaison would be necessary.

Captain Shortland touched his wounded arm. "Pity about that," he said. "You won't be able to make tea for a few weeks. Still, you're lucky the man wasn't aiming at your chest."

In barely a minute, a colonel, followed by several high-ranking officers, strode into the office. They informed Shortland that a jury of twelve farmers had been brought to the prison together with a coroner. An account of the action, together with depositions from British soldiers and American prisoners would be presented to them. Adams was ordered to stay and help with the depositions.

Lieutenants Avelyne and Fortye and Ensign White, the three junior officers who had remained at dinner throughout the action, stated that it was irregular for a naval officer to take command of soldiers and that when they had not been sent for they had assumed they had been relieved of their authority and had therefore continued with their meal.

Charles Andrews said that what he had gone through would give him nightmares for the rest of his life, and Captain Shortland was the evil devil who had schemed it.

Dr McGrath said he felt the carnage had been unnecessary; the bloodshed had been horrifying; although he admitted that Captain Shortland had tried to stop the bayonet fighting.

159

The sergeant of the firing-squad agreed that he had been hesitant in obeying the captain's orders because the prisoners were unarmed and were civilians.

The depositions continued for hours, and the coroner and jury reached the conclusion that the deaths of nine men had been caused through homicide.

"In that case, Captain Shortland," said the colonel, "I must ask you to surrender to me your sword and pistols, and to consider yourself under arrest until a court martial can be convened some time in the morning. In future, the Americans will not be referred to as prisoners but as repatriates. The garrison will hand over their musketry to the ammunition store and will patrol unarmed. I shall assume command of this establishment, and shall make my headquarters in a building outside the gate. Good day to you sir!"

Shortland burst out laughing after the colonel had left. "I'm the only prisoner in Dartmoor – by George, that's as amusing as your *Beggar's Opera*, Mr Adams. I'll tell you what, I'll make a cup of tea for both of us, being as how you can't use your arms. And then I'll have to sit down and write out my last will and testament. Trouble is, Mr Adams, I've no next of kin, and I've nothing to leave them if I had. Oh, I tell a lie, I have an aunt in Surrey. Everybody has an aunt in Surrey; I'm surprised you don't; I'm sure you'd find one if you delved into it. I can leave her my painting up there. She's never seen me and she'd be rather proud, what?"

"Are you serious?"

"Good heavens, never more serious, Mr Adams! Your government and my government will demand it in order to balance the ledger. I shall be found guilty – and shot."

160

CHAPTER TEN

A Cold Fire, A Dark Sun, A Dry Sea, An Ungood God

THE Somersetshire Militia had a brass band, and a fine brass band it was. They played all the country airs – 'Pedlar Jim', 'Blow Away the Morning Dew', 'Early One Morning' and their own 'Dashing Away with the Smoothing Iron'. It was as gay as a carnival outside the office where Captain Shortland was facing his court martial. An American colonel, Charles King, and an English admiral, Seymour Larpent, had been appointed as joint presidents, and the rest of the court was divided equally between British and American officers.

As each witness left the office, he made a throat-cut gesture with his hand to his neck, or put his fingers to his head and pretended his thumb was a trigger. It sickened John, for Shortland was doomed and the merriment was exactly as he had once experienced in Exeter for a hanging. He was the last man to be called as a witness.

The officers looked like hungry hawks. Behind them was the Union Jack and the Stars and Stripes. Shortland's sword lay on the table, but Shortland was not present. It was as if the court were judging the sword and not the man.

"Would you give the court your assessment of Captain Shortland?" asked the admiral.

"As an administrator he was able and fair-minded. As a man he showed humanity and humour."

"Tell me," said the American colonel, "what would have happened had the Americans overcome the garrison?"

"Simple. We would have taken over the prison."

"Is it not rather ridiculous to assume that unarmed men could overcome a regiment of the line?" asked the admiral.

161

"The Americans outnumbered the British by five to one."

"But they were unarmed."

"Some were armed."

"I understand the Americans merely wanted their ball back," said the American colonel with a wry smile.

"They wanted their freedom back," said Adams. "The Americans were being kept in prison in spite of a peace treaty guaranteeing their release. There was disease and food ran out. They felt they were doomed, and they were taunted by the soldiers."

"Are you implying there was a lack of discipline in the British regiment?" asked the admiral.

"They were in the same boat."

"Don't you mean prison?"

"The British and the Americans felt betrayed by their own governments. They were walled up in a granite dungeon on an unknown moor, and they were conveniently forgotten about. They could rot."

"The United States had neither the ships nor the finances to repatriate its unfortunate prisoners," said the American colonel.

"And the British government was far too occupied defending Britain from Napoleon," said the admiral.

"And so Captain Shortland is on trial for making the best of a bad job?" asked John Adams.

"Captain Shortland is on trial for murder," chipped in a junior American officer.

"Nine deaths, Mr Adams. Just think on it – nine deaths," a British officer said quietly.

"It's nine deaths too many, gentlemen; but Captain Shortland's audacious action prevented a massacre from becoming a holocaust."

"Would you explain to the court?"

"The Americans backed away and dispersed because Captain Shortland displayed his authority. He used fifteen soldiers. He could have commanded a thousand muskets and six cannons. The British eventually stood off because they realised Captain Shortland stood between them and their being torn to pieces to a man by the Americans. It was a touch-and-go situation."

"Are you seriously suggesting that a mob, a rabble, could have overwhelmed a well-trained regiment of soldiers?"

"I believe it was done in the War of Independence, and more recently at New Orleans."

"In your territory, not ours," said the admiral. "In this prison there are no fields to run in, no woods to hide in."

"Our losses would have been heavy, but by sheer arithmetic we would have overcome the soldiers."

"And what would you have done then?"

"We might, just might, have marched down to Tor Quay and captured the *Bellerophon*. The world would then have heard the name of Dartmoor Prison. However, Captain Shortland unwittingly foiled that action. In my opinion, sirs, it was an American victory with the loss of only nine men, similar to Concord."

"How do you make out it was a victory?"

"Because it brought to the attention of both governments the plight of four to five thousand forgotten men. You may execute Captain Shortland if you want a scapegoat, but you can't execute five thousand men, who are mainly civilians. You will have to do something about us now, whether you like it or not."

"Some ball game – eh, Mr Adams?" said the American colonel.

The admiral coughed. It was not amusing. "I see that you were wounded in the action," he said. "You were obviously with your countrymen at the time. Do you consider Captain Shortland's action was justified?"

"I bitterly regret the deaths of my countrymen, just as I regret the many deaths over the past three years. Nevertheless, I consider Captain Shortland was justified. May I remind you gentlemen of what you saw over the main gate."

"I saw the Stars and Stripes," said the colonel.

"And I saw the British flag," said the admiral.

"Between both flags was an inscription of Virgil's – 'Parcere Subjectis' – 'Show mercy to the vanquished'."

"You may step down."

John returned to the office to wait for the verdict. After what seemed an age, the door opened and Captain Shortland walked in with his sword in his hand.

"Wouldn't you think, Mr Adams that when somebody borrows my sword they would have the goodness to keep it clean? I think they've been cutting cake with it."

"You're aquitted?"

"Justifiable homicide. A unanimous verdict."

"I'll make tea. One-handed."

"Do."

"I shall inform the prisoners."

"Prisoners, Mr Adams? Where on earth did you pick up such a quaint term? They're repatriates. Repatriates."

"I shall inform the repatriates, sir."

"And you might call a parade for eight o'clock tomorrow morning. I've some important news for them."

The Yankees grudgingly assembled in the main yard the following morning. They kept better and straighter ranks than did the Somersetshire Militia who flanked them on either side. They didn't trust Captain Shortland or the British soldiery, and as a precaution most men held rocks behind their backs. Captain Shortland stepped to the front of the parade. John Adams called "Attention" to the Americans; the Somersetshire sergeants called "Attention" to their men.

The band struck up Carey's 'God Save the King' and the Americans, in their own free time, in disorder and with jeers, lolled at ease. Many turned their backs and John felt sympathy for them, so soon after the riot and the killings and the court martial.

Captain Shortland ignored the break in ranks. "I have news for the repatriates," he said. "The British government has agreed to pay half the costs of repatriation, and to place British ships at the disposal of the States of America for transportation. All ships confiscated during the recent hostilities will be returned to their owners and masters immediately, and they will be compensated for any damage. The first draft of three hundred men will leave here for Plymouth in two days' time. Thereafter, there will be a similar embarkation draft each week. Meanwhile, you are the guests of King George the Third."

164

The men who yesterday were hoping for the captain's execution now cheered and yelled "Good Old Shitland!" and "Good Old Shortarse!" and other pet names they had for him. They cheered and wept.

Captain Shortland turned to the regimental band and signalled them to play. They began a tune that John remembered from Harvard. It was a drinking song about the Greek poet Anacreon, a lover of wine, woman and song, going through the gates of heaven. He wondered why Shortland should have chosen such an obscure song, but he didn't have to wonder for long.

"That, gentleman, for what it is worth, is the national song of your country. I shall ask the band to play it again."

The band played it again, and the men shyly found they could sing the words they'd learned to it:

"Oh, say can you see by the dawn's early light,
What so proudly we hail in the twilight's fast gleaming."

They dropped the rocks behind their backs, stood to attention and eyed their country's flag over the main gate.

"O thus be it ever when free men shall stand
Between their loved home and the war's desolation;
Blest with victory and peace, may the heaven-rescued land
Praise the power that hath made and preserved us a nation."

The majority of men sniffed and wiped their eyes with their sleeves, although there were quite a few hundred who just sobbed aloud. The Somersetshire Militia band saved embarrassment by bursting into the tune of the Jolly Miller who lived on the River Dee.

Afterwards the Americans broke ranks and sang 'Yankee Doodle'.

Then came a new sound: the bells of St Michael's, the church built stone by tough stone by the Yankees. It was pealing a merry summons to its altar for its first service.

John thought of the American colonel's remark – "Some ball game, eh?" – and he was about to join the rush to the church.

165

And what was that rejoinder of Shortland's? "Build a church or the devil will make pagans of us all on Dartmoor!" No chance; no more could Dartmoor lose itself in eternal mists. Shortland stopped him. "There's no need for you to go, Mr Adams," he said. "The vicar has told me all about his first service. There's that psalm about the waters of Babylon, and how on earth can you sing the Lord's song in a strange land? And there's a fairly new hymn about the rock of ages – might have been written about these tors, mmm? There y'are, I've saved you half an hour's travelling time to reach that little beauty you've tucked away in the hills. Oh yes, I saw you kissing her that day you put on that stupid opera; she's a little gem. So take horse, bring her back and marry her in your church before the vicar returns to heaven or Plymouth or wherever. Marry her in your Yankee church. Don't stand here talking to me, man!"

"Yes, sir! I mean no, sir!"

"Ay, three bags full. You should be there by now!"

John wasted no time. He ran through the main street of Princetown, grabbed his white horse from Mother Goose's, jumped on its back and galloped out of town as though the fiends were after him.

> "I roved from fair to fair,
>   Likewise from town to town,
>   Until I married me a wife,
>   And the world turned upside-down."

He was as free and as happy as a skylark. His horse shuffled through the heather as though it wore carpet slippers. Occasionally a hoof chinked and flung sparks as it struck light-grey granite. This was Pegasus; it flew between the tors.

At last it halted before Sally's stone cottage. John jumped off, stumbled and nearly fell, so excited was he.

The cottage was derelict. He couldn't believe it. It was empty. The fire had long since gone out and the hearth was swept clean. The shelves were all empty -- not a jar, not a flagon. The table, the chairs, the bed, all gone. Sally had vanished into thin air. No, she couldn't have gone. She *was* the moor, the moor at its most

166

loveliest, the moor at its most capricious. To say she had gone was to say Dartmoor had gone, the prison had gone, and the yellow gorse, the stubbled grass, the heather, the crags, the ravens, the ponies, the foxes, the lonely forget-me-not between the two crags. No, she couldn't have gone. But she had. The world was turned inside-out not upside-down.

"Sally! Sally!" he shouted her name repeatedly. He searched the cottage for some trace of her as a bloodhound sniffs a trail. There was nothing to show that Sally had ever set up home in the cottage, neither hairpin nor penny; it was swept clean. He wandered around the circle of stones; but they had lost their magic, they were just stones.

"Sally! Sally!" He called her name in the heather in all directions, and shouted up to the tors. The stockade was empty, the horses had gone. He was in a strange land.

He decided to curl up in a corner of what had been the bedroom. Maybe she would return in the night, or maybe he would be whisked away by whatever had whisked her away. It was what the ancients called a vigil, keeping watch through the night and praying, only he couldn't pray, he could only think.

He knew why she had deserted him. She had deserted him because he'd refused the *Bellerophon* adventure. How could she know that all had been achieved? Her last words had been to call him a coward, but she didn't know that. She didn't know how his mind had been forced to fight. Bravery wasn't all like the fighting cocks at Chagford, but she wasn't to know. Her terms were simple and innocent.

Nothing happened. Daylight was early. The sky was blood red over the distant sea; some of the tors due east were lit up as though on fire. Sally had not appeared by magic. There was no magic to Sally, she was just Sally – and he had lost her.

He walked most of the way back to Dartmoor Prison. There was nothing else to do, and soon this very prison, his home for over three years, was going to desert him.

He even sang a song which could be a hymn to Sally:

> "My master and the neighbours all
> Make game of me and Sally,

167

And but for her, I'd better be
A slave and row a galley;
But when my seven long years are out,
O then I'll marry Sally;
O then we'll wed, and then we'll bed –
But not in our alley.''

The words of the song hurt him and he punched one fist into
the other.

CHAPTER ELEVEN

A Bird out of the Snare

DARTMOOR citadel in the midsummer sunshine was golden, and the granite tors were golden. They could have been castles waved into shape and being by a wind-fast, wind-whispering Merlin. When the sun made love to the moor, and lit up the bright yellow gorse and pink heather, it was an enchanted land. To John it was the sinister, throbbing, curling, musical, breathing land of Spencer's *Faerie Queen*. It had dwarfs, knee-stepping palfreys, lances for the love of a lady, the coloured shields of King Arthur, with Camelot always over and beyond the next hill. It was a giant book of poetry, unreal, bewitching; and he rode daily over it, always calling at Sally's cottage, which was always empty. Sally was always over and beyond the next hill.

There were now about a hundred men left in the prison. John and Captain Shortland had taken rooms in the Plume of Feathers, where John's fist was rarely short of a tankard of ale. Few traders were left in Princetown; the Jew of Dartmoor had long since cleared his debt.

John's ship, the *Boston Trader*, was lying berthed in the port of Exmouth. It was being victualled for the trip by John's appointed first mate, Charles Andrews, and it had been agreed to carry some of the repatriates as passengers.

"Cheer up, skipper!" said Shortland. "You're going home. Don't tell me you've become an Englishman."

"I'm a Yankee. But I've got no home."

"You'll soon find one. They tell me every man who goes to America finds his own America."

"If he has the right wife. I've lost that chance."

"Poor John Adams. Lost his heart to an Englishwoman!"

"She's from Cornwall."

"Trelawny people, eh? Land of the Irish saints. Used to be rebellious, but they're docile enough now."

"Are they?" John laughed with the irony of it all.

"Well," said Shortland, getting up and draining his pot, "we'd better go and shut up shop. They were going to give me one of those new-fangled broughams to take me to Exeter, but who wants to ride covered in this weather? Besides, it's the last time I'll breathe the moorland air. I said no, send me a pochay. At least you can ride with me."

"Thank you."

The two men strolled across to the empty prison. Doors creaked on their hinges, ravens searched the yards for scraps, a frightened fox ran out of one of the cell blocks. John felt lonely. He didn't want to leave the prison.

He and the captain took down their countries' flags, folded them and took them across to the church for safekeeping. Shortland looked back. Maybe he too didn't want to leave the prison.

" 'And thorns shall come up in her palaces, nettles and brambles in the fortresses thereof: and it shall be an habitation of dragons, and a court for owls, and satyrs shall dance there.' Mmm! You might think Isaiah had been a Yankee prisoner – eh, John?" said Shortland. He stopped beneath the arch which read *Parcere Subjectis* and shrugged his shoulders.

"Ah well, we did our best."

"And we leave two hundred and fifty-two Yankees buried within the walls," added John. "Smallpox, lung diseases, African fever, suicides and murders."

"Including nine men on my conscience," said Shortland. "It's something I've got to live with."

John hitched the white horse to the rear of the post-chaise.

"You're taking that horse with you to America?"

"It's all I've got left."

"What's its name?"

"Sometimes I call it Prince, after the patron of our prison, but I've not given it a permanent name as yet. I may call it Captain."

"After me? I'm honoured."

170

"Jointly between you and Captain Cotgrave."

"Well, you might say 'sir' to it occasionally."

"Yes, sir."

"You were right, you know. Dartmoor was an American victory."

"That was just law-room rhetoric."

"Was it? I'm not so sure. Over the past three or four years flags have been going up and down flagpoles like monkeys on a stick, but your flag has remained flying. And your men have returned with skills your country needs, and your boys have gone back with an education. And in all those years only a few men brought discredit to your nation."

"Thank you!"

"And you had a small share in another victory."

"Oh?"

"I heard a bit of news about your Virginian Highlanders," said Shortland.

John acknowledged the remark with just a grunt. He had ceased being surprised by the captain's revelations; he had known of every scheme the prisoners had tried out; he had known about the opera whores and the capture of a fishing fleet.

"Yes, indeed," went on Shortland. "They ran. At Waterloo."

"Oh, God," said John. "The only reason they joined up with the British Army was to redeem themselves after running in Canada."

"Oh yes, they ran like hell. It seems they held on to the stirrups of the cavalry. I would guess their paces to have been about ten feet wide. And they dropped off behind the French lines, which rather surprised the French. Not strictly according to the rules and regulations of organised warfare, of course. However, most of them were commended for their bravery, and Sergeant Cotton was promoted to the rank of major on the field by none other than the Duke of Wellington himself. And that at Waterloo, which rather justifies my allowing you to carry on with the prisoner exchange. Unfortunately, Major Cotton and his Highlanders have disappeared, so he's in for a court martial when found."

"Which he won't be," said John. "He'll be back home chasing the buffalo."

171

The scenery changed as suddenly as though a straight line had been drawn between the bleak moorland and the luscious countryside of Devonshire. It became the England which most New Englanders imagined when they heard the tune of 'Greensleeves'. Cottages were painted white, pink and green and they were all topped with light-brown thatched roofs. Their gardens were overflowing with red, yellow and purple flowers; the chestnut trees were covered in cream-coloured blossom, and the elderberry trees wore the dainty white lace of a bride. The woman carried large wicker shopping baskets with lettuce and fish and loaves peeping over the rims, and the men lounged and smoked their long pipes. The meadows were sweet green and dotted with sheep; the soil was red, and the sheep had red blotches on their whiteness from off the soil. The hills were smooth and round, and there were no rocks. As the carriage drove through woodland, deer stopped and turned their heads square to the carriage, regardless of the direction of their bodies. Eventually through the trees John saw the estuary of the Exe with a hundred masts sticking up from it. And he saw the two towers of the cathedral coming towards him. The towers were not bishops, they were druids, blown upon by moorland night winds; they knew the answers to questions that nobody dared to ask.

He did not trust the cathedral, and was glad when it went behind the carriage. Captain Shortland bid him adieu at Topsham, and his carriage sped away, leaving John to find the *Boston Trader*. It didn't take him long to find her, but the dream of three years was a disappointment. He felt no thrill as he stepped aboard.

"All shipshape and Bristol fashion," reported Charles Andrews.

The ship was indeed clean; she had been kept in good trim. It was as though the *Boston Trader* had made herself beautiful in order to please her estranged master, but to John she was just a ship, not nearly as beautiful as those carved out of bone and wood by the prisoners.

The longboat with its crew of oarsmen was already secured to the ship in readiness to pull her out into the mainstream on the ebb.

Suddenly all the men who had been busy with the sails and the ropes around the capstans, and the men in the longboat, stopped and stared in one direction. Some whistled.

A young woman rode on to the quayside. She rode side-saddle in the manner of an elegant lady. Elegance! Everything about her was elegant. She wore a green velvet costume and a green velvet cocked hat. The buckles on her shoes shone like gold. Her earrings flashed in the light, as did her eyes. She slid off the horse noiselessly and walked over the gangplank. It was Sally.

John was open-mouthed and speechless.

"Can you provide passage for one lady and her horse? I can pay you handsomely."

"But . . . I . . . er . . . when . . . if you . . . away," spluttered John.

"I thought you were going to take me across the Mississippi and show me them chicasaws and feed me on buffalo. Course, if you've changed your mind – " She turned as though to return to the gangplank.

"If you attempt to leave this ship," said John, "I'll clap you in irons. You're my prisoner." Then he became serious. "Why did you disappear? I was almost driven mad."

"Oh John, you're so impractical. I had to sell everything I possessed at Exeter market. My horses and everything. The wines had to go, because you wouldn't want them ravens getting drunk on my elderberry, and you wouldn't want wild ponies getting themselves a-covered in sticky jam, and can you imagine foxes and rabbits sitting at the table?"

"Or wild ponies going to bed?" laughed John.

Some mariners brought her horse on board and stabled it in the same stabling they had constructed on deck for John's horse.

"Oh darling, welcome to my very beautiful ship!" said John.

"'Tis bigger than the one you gave me. Oh, and I've placed all the money in the bank and obtained letters of authority."

They spoke no more, for John put his arm round her and kissed her, to an accompaniment of whistles. They didn't hear Charles Andrews's commands.

"Hoist fore-course and stand by the yards!"

"Ay, ay!"

"Let go for'ard!"

"Ay, ay!"

"Let go aft!"

"For'ard and aft free!"

"Let go yawl, and trim the yards!"

"Excuse me, captain!"

"What's that?"

"I said excuse me, captain. We're under way, and it should be your duty to break the flag."

Still with his arm around Sally, John gave the command: "Break the flag free!"

Reluctantly at first, the Stars and Stripes dropped from the mizen-mast and then, as the wind took it, it flapped and unfurled. A British frigate in the estuary fired a salute.